PRESENCE OF MY ENEMIES

Christopher Gladu

D1565399

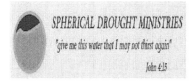

SPHERICAL DROUGHT MINISTRIES

"give me this water that I may not thirst again"

John 4:15

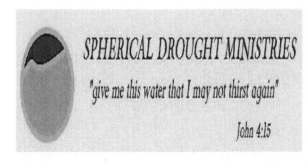

SPHERICAL DROUGHT MINISTRIES

"give me this water that I may not thirst again"

John 4:15

Spherical Drought Ministries
ATTN: Permissions
P.O. BOX 564, Seffner, FL 33583

http://www.sphericaldrought.org

ISBN 9781452860893

Cover art: *"We can get through this," oil on canvas by Chris Gladu*

Dedication

This book is dedicated to my Lord and Savior Jesus Christ and to a special teenage girl living in the Roman province of Palestine during the Augustinian census. Her faithful decision to trust God in the face of a difficult situation not only gave us the perfect example of how to deal with an unplanned pregnancy, but also changed the history of the world for all time. One girl saying, "Yes" to life can do that.

I also dedicate this work to my sacramental sweetheart Guadalupe, who is the most incredible wife and mother I know, and to my beautiful daughters, Marianne Victoria and Ashtoun Shantell, as well as all the sidewalk counselors, pregnancy center volunteers, NFP instructors and prayer warriors who try to make a difference by loving mothers and babies in crisis.

Author's Acknowledgements

I would like to express my gratitude to all those who made this book possible. First and foremost to my editor, Phil Finan, whose command of grammar and mastery of the written word helped to transform this manuscript into what it is.

I'd like to thank Cari Carpenter who was my coach and sounding board, providing steadfast encouragement and invaluable suggestions throughout the creative process.

I offer special thanks to Patti Toler for giving me the benefit of her experience with her professional advice and punctuation skills as well as April-Dawn Gladu for her advice on formatting and Guadalupe Gladu for her help with general editing.

I extend my gratitude to all of my reviewers for their feedback and assistance: Elizabeth Baker, John Biel, Kathy Brasseur, Mercedes Figueroa, Karen Garnett, Danielle Garcia-Jones, Melissa Jones, Sheila Hopkins, Jeff Joaquin, Maureen Kubasky, Jack Lavery, Joe Malyk, Stephanie Martin, Brandy Orphanides, Sarah Shea, Jacqueline Winter.

"Religion that is pure and undefiled before God the Father is this: to care for orphans and widows in their affliction and to keep oneself unstained by the world."

James 1:27

Prologue

"AAAHHhhhhhhhh … hh …," Tammy's last breath slipped away as her heart stopped beating. Alone now in her thoughts, she couldn't hear the artificial respirator pumping oxygen into a body that no longer required it. Although she had no sight, she was aware of her surroundings, which gave her comfort.

The pain is gone, she thought to herself. Even without the ability to hear, speak, or see, she was unafraid, no longer bound by the limits of the five senses or negative emotions – such as fear – that cloud the perceptions of people still trapped in linear time. Now that she realized how things all fit together, everything was much clearer, and she felt more peaceful than she had imagined.

I died in a state of grace, but I'm still too attached to sin to stand in His presence. I know that He is not here with me exactly, but that once I address my imperfections, I'll be ready. I want that because I love Him, and I want to give myself to Him clean and prepared. Once I am with Him I can intercede for my loved ones, who are struggling to get here but are still trapped in time, she thought. All of this was instantly clear and made total sense as she saw her role in the Divine vision and wanted to fulfill it.

Another presence joined her. No actual words were exchanged; language did not exist here – just the knowing of the presence and heart of another. The exchange was instant, as time had no meaning in eternity; they communicated in the moment.

Tammy, I'm Gabe, and I'm here to ease your transition. By the way, congratulations, you are no longer capable of sinning because your will is now completing its transformation into His will. He wants you to join with Him in His beatific vision for eternity, but first you need to examine a period in your life that has caused you to be here rather than at your final destination. We need to review those events so that you can forgive and be ready to share in His presence. To achieve the final purification, we must first go back to examine the pain that led to these occasions of sin. Let's begin with that first pregnancy when you were a teenager …

"I don't see why it has to be this way!" Tammy yelled at the habited religious in front of her. "Why can't I keep my baby?"

"What kind of a life could you offer this child? She would just be a poor fatherless child and looked down on by everybody," Sister retorted. "Everyone would know what you did! Hasn't your mother been through enough without an unwanted child bringing more suffering? What kind of life would this child have? Stop thinking so selfishly!" Sister Shiphrah's words cut deep into Tammy's already wounded heart. Tammy's father had run off with his secretary and had left her mother with Tammy and her two little brothers and no visible means of support. Sister Shiphrah knew this. While the Church had helped the family with groceries and second-hand clothing, socially, Tammy's family members were considered pariahs, and few respectable women would have anything to do with her mother for years. Even the nuns at her school treated Tammy with disdain because her father had left. Some parents forbade their children to associate with Tammy or her brothers outside of school. It was as if they all wore a scarlet letter – except her father, who was now happily remarried and living in another state.

When Tammy started dating, she was not educated in how to have healthy relationships with the opposite sex. So with limited knowledge, she plunged into a relationship without knowing how to set boundaries. Growing up without a father in the home had caused her natural need for love and attention from men to express itself in a disordered way. Her stay at the convent was the result of making the wrong decision about premarital sex in a misguided effort to feel accepted and loved.

"None of this would have happened if you hadn't been running around like a floozy! Have you no shame?" Sister Shiphrah said. She showed no pity for what she considered undisciplined girls. The young women tossed aside their moral upbringing and embarrassed their parents to the point where the parents sent their daughters to a convent until the babies were born. The babies were placed for adoption with couples who could not have biological children, and everyone was better off for it. After the births, the girls would return home with made-up stories about taking care of a sick aunt or needing to be in a quiet setting to improve their studies, or similar lies that would cover their parents' shame for having raised such immoral girls.

"But why can't I see her? Why can't I hold my baby?" cried Tammy.

"Get it into your head now, girl! A baby needs a mother and a father – married parents to raise her in a morally fit home. Your promiscuity not only shamed your family but God too." Tammy knew that she would not be allowed to see the baby. That had been one of the conditions of giving birth at the convent. Now all she wanted was to see and hold the child. They said it had been a girl ... she had a daughter. Lying there, she could hear the baby's cries from the other room where Sister Puha was probably cleaning her up and getting her ready to go to the orphanage. Tammy had been restrained on the birthing table during labor – she thought that maybe it was for leverage – but now she knew the real reason. Tammy knew she would have launched herself off that table and through the door and grabbed her child and not let go. "I hate you, you old witch!" Tammy screamed at Sister Shiphrah.

"May God forgive you, and guide you along the right path so to straighten yourself out and act responsibly," Sister Shiphrah replied stonily. "Maybe you'll be lucky and get a halfway decent man – someone out of prison who's reformed!" It was at that moment when Tammy knew pure hatred. She realized that she would never see her newborn daughter. Her mother had already signed away Tammy's parental rights since she was her legal guardian. It was all official now and she was going to have to live with the fact that she would never see her daughter. The sobs came in streams as she, exhausted and overwhelmed, cried herself to sleep.

Sister Shiphrah left the room and joined the other religious in the nursery. "She's sleeping now, Puha. She's exhausted. She'll be out for a couple of hours for sure. Has the van been called?"

'The van' was a reference to the sisters who came to take the newborns to the orphanage in the city. In this case, they would need to do it before Tammy could be released from her restraints. They never told the girls where the orphanage was, as most of the girls came from far away, and it was easier for the families who needed cover stories to salvage their reputations.

"Let me hold the child," said Shiphrah, taking the infant from Puha. Despite her rigid and inflexible exterior, Sister Shiphrah had a huge heart for the babies. She had been born, Mary Francis Dooley, but had taken the religious name, Shiphrah, after one of the Egyptian midwives who had saved Moses in the book of Exodus. Her sister religious Puha had done the same. She had grown up as Marie-Laure Benoit in a wealthy family who had everything, yet her calling to serve the needs of unwed mothers and children had been very strong. With that, she took on the toughest possible name as a penance in reparation for the sins against chastity committed by those in her care.

The world as they knew it, both in society and within the Church, was changing rapidly. It was rumored that the Mother Superior was in California; she was meeting with leaders of other religious orders who had just undergone a phenomenological spirituality seminar with a famous humanistic psychologist. Shiphrah and Puha had heard that the Order might discontinue wearing the habits – something they couldn't imagine happening. Perhaps some of the younger sisters would be more enthusiastic about the change but Shiphrah and Puha were from the old school and didn't like change. They did not join the Order of Our Lady's Handmaidens because they wanted change and excitement. The convent, their mission, the daily disciplines, the reading of the Divine Office, the habit, all of it was significant to them. Although their Order had been blessed with many young vocations over the last few years – the fruit of the so-called baby boom after the Second World War – change, they thought, was not good. But instead of voicing their opinions, the women just turned their feelings over to God and their superiors.

There was a knock at the door and Shiphrah, holding a lit candle in the dim hallway, went to answer it. Ralph, a clean, well-dressed, older man came in and removed his hat. Along with him were Sister Simeone and the social worker from the orphanage.

"Please Ralph, do come in," Sister Shiphrah said.

"Thank you, Sister. This is Mr. Orphelin from State Social Services. He's here to take the baby into foster care. And of course you know Sister Simeone," Ralph replied.

"Good evening, Shiphrah," said Sister Simeone ... Shiphrah dropped her candle on the floor in shock.

"Oh!" she gasped, and bent down to pick up the candle, which fortunately had extinguished itself in its own wax drippings before it hit the wood floor. "Simeone, your habit!" Shiphrah exclaimed. "What happened?"

Before her, stood a woman she had known since professing her first set of vows twenty years ago, but she had never seen her like this: her short hair was completely exposed, and her outfit made her look like the checkout girl at the local grocery store – except for the extra-large crucifix, which she wore prominently around her neck. Something else was different too – she was wearing make-up.

After the initial shock, Shiphrah said, "Foster care? What about the orphanage? When I spoke to you on the phone, Sister Simeone, you didn't mention anything about foster care."

Mr. Orphelin said, "Through state-funded research, we have determined that raising children in a more home-like atmosphere with foster parents will help orphans be better adjusted to family life once they are adopted. Your Order has contracted with the state to provide the services to the unwed pregnant girls while we take over with raising the children. By selling some of the buildings now used for the orphanage, we can use the savings to help compensate the families that participate in our program."

"So instead of having a charitable orphanage where they are all raised together, they will be placed with families who are paid to take care of them?" Sister Puha asked dubiously. "How is that better?"

"It's a new world, Sister, and everything is changing, and I am just a part of the new system," he smiled blankly and took the infant from her arms. "What should we call her while she's in the system? We need to put a name on the preliminary birth certificate."

"How about Ruth?" Simeone suggested. In subsequent years, many children would get their first names in this arbitrary manner. "I'm sorry for shocking you this way, Shiphrah. I almost made you burn the house down! When we spoke on the phone I should have mentioned that our Province is rolling out the changes that the Motherhouse adopted out in California."

Tammy awoke, still tied to the bed, but she had been cleaned up. She remembered everything and felt helpless in the face of her circumstances. Lying there, she felt emotionally drained. Still unable to get up, she emptied her bladder on the delivery table. "Let those witches deal with that!" she sobbed. "I'm so sorry for giving in to David's advances. It was wrong, and I wish I had never done it, but this pain of separation from my child is unbearable. And these nuns, they knew what they were doing! They tricked me! I hate them, and I will never forgive them."

Tammy heard Gabe speak in her heart. "You have held this anger and never really let go of it. It is the reason why you are in purgation instead of with the One who loves you. Are you ready to forgive? Are you ready to accept forgiveness?"

I. A Day in the Life

Chapter 1

TIME: "Now"

"Dang! He said he'd be here waiting for me!" Rachel screamed out loud. No one else could hear her because her car windows were closed, and the radio was cranked up. Rachel just parked her car and began indulging in a personal meltdown, while at the same time, a shrill young woman's voice on the radio belted out angry words in surround-sound. *"...Men are the problem, me I can do without..."* Rachel loved music and often found expression for all of her feelings in song lyrics. At this moment, she was trying desperately to find courage in them to avoid thinking about the major roadblock she might be facing to all of her plans.

Rachel came from a solid family. Solid enough anyway or at least that's what she told herself. True, she had never known her biological father, and her mom was on her third husband, but mom had been with this guy for five years now, which was long-term where her mother was concerned. He had a nice family with parents whom she called Grandma and Grandpa that lived close by and usually brought homemade treats when they came to visit. They were much nicer than the messed up people that her mom's previous husbands had brought into their lives – particularly the second husband's brother, who had molested her. All three of her younger sisters had different fathers but called their mom's current husband 'Dad' – at least when they wanted something.

Rachel's mom had taught them how to manipulate men. To Rachel, this was natural, and she did it without even thinking about it. Men were a vehicle for getting whatever she wanted, whether it was pleasure, a free meal, attention, approval, or gifts. Rachel knew she was a desirable young woman, and she was willing to give men what they wanted as a tradeoff.

In an effort to be proactive, and for Rachel's protection, her mother had started her on the pill as soon as she turned

1

fourteen. Taking her daily dose was as automatic as getting her first cup of coffee. She had been doing it successfully for six years, through three relationships and several other discreet encounters. Only this time, with the pressure of finals and all night study sessions, she had forgotten.

"Dang!" Rachel yelled. Her current boyfriend Tom was supposed to have been here already. This is why she was waiting for him in the parking lot of the abortion clinic.

Rachel kept singing along with the radio because the tone and the mood of the song perfectly fit her state of mind. After the song ended and Tom still wasn't there, the tears began.

"It isn't fair! I've always been good! I've always taken my dang pill like clockwork, and this is my reward for being responsible! Bull!" Rachel yelled into empty air. She was here for a pregnancy test because she didn't believe the three positive drugstore tests she had taken at home. The label had read '*Pharmska Pregnancy Test: The most accurate value pregnancy test you can buy,*' that was probably just marketing, she reasoned. Since all three tests were from the same manufacturer, she figured the kits were defective; at least that's what she was hoping. Although she was very nervous, Rachel knew she'd hear those stress-free words spoken by the doctor, "You're not pregnant. It was just a false alarm."

When she made the appointment, Rachel was told the test was $50, and the clinic only took cash. Rachel figured this test would be better since it cost more and of course, Tom would pay for it since he paid for everything. She thought that Tom was kind of a wimpy guy, not in the physical sense, but in who he was. He was always so indecisive and could easily be swayed into doing whatever someone else wanted.

Rachel didn't love Tom, but he was so easy going that it was a very comfortable relationship – for now. Plus, the fact that Tom always had money to spend on her made being with him that much easier. Tom, on the other hand, was madly in love with Rachel. She was his first serious girlfriend, and he often spoke of his long-term plan to marry her, even though they had only been together since the start of the semester. Tom worshiped her and

2

would do anything to get her approval. That's why it was so surprising that he wasn't here yet. This wasn't something she wanted to do alone, especially in a run-down neighborhood. A mechanical version of a song called "Just a Loser" began to play. It was Rachel's cell phone, and that was the song that she had set up as her alert that Tom was texting her. The tune had no meaning to Tom, but Rachel's girlfriends all knew what the song meant, and one of them even took to humming it whenever she was around Tom and Rachel. Little did Tom know that he was just one in a line of many men Rachel used for her own purposes, and that she would dump him when he was no longer convenient. Rachel checked her phone and read the message.

"SORY BABE PROF GRABD ME AFT CLASS CAN'T BE THERE LUV U." Rachel cursed to herself for not telling him why she had the doctor's appointment. Now she had to figure out if she had the $50 since Tom wouldn't be here to pay for it. She began to check her purse, glove compartment, and the hiding place where she usually kept emergency gas money. Letting out a sigh, she had a total of $52, so that meant she could buy a soda afterwards too. "Stupid jerk – making me come out here by myself! You're NOT getting any tonight!" she said out loud to make herself feel better. It helped for a second but then she just felt alone, really alone, and more than just a little scared.

It was getting stuffy in the car. The Chrysler LeBaron had seen better days than this one. The window was fogging up the cracks, which divided the foggy segments from the clear ones in the windshield. It was time to go inside and get the test over with so she could relax again. Exiting her car, she ignored the loud creek of the door. Rachel was careful not to touch the candy-red Jaguar parked next to her. She couldn't help noticing it – it was her dream car, right down to the hot Florida vanity plate that read 'NOT REDY.' Rachel had to lift her car door slightly to get it to shut, as the door would drop an inch when it was opened. When she slammed it shut, the door didn't catch, and the driver's side arm rest fell onto the driver's seat – a testament to the inefficiency of super glue and duct tape.

"Let me try," a woman's voice said from behind her, and before she could say anything, a lady appeared and gave the door a quick push. SLAM! It closed.

3

"I hate Chryslers too," said this Good Samaritan, turning around to reveal the face of the most beautiful woman Rachel had ever seen. "I'm Lucy, they're waiting for you inside, Rachel. Just follow the sidewalk, and pay no attention to those hateful protesters lined up along the fence."

Rachel was spellbound by this woman's beauty. Lucy was about 5'5" and had the perfect figure that all men craved and all women envied. Somehow, she was both curvaceous and slim at the same time. Her blonde hair was long with a slight wave, and every feature on her face was perfectly symmetrical. Her eyes – there was something mysterious and terrifying about her eyes. Rachel thought they looked like they had no pupils and no whites – *but that was impossible.* There was something deeply disturbing about them. It was as if they were looking into Rachel's soul as they penetrated all her normal defenses. Lucy wore an expensive blue dress with a plunging neckline that showed cleavage, a white belt with matching heels, and tasteful 24-karat gold earrings with a little peace symbol on them. *No, it wasn't a peace symbol, but one of those yin-yang ornaments.* Around her neck, she sported a golden cross that was shaped more like a question mark with a bar across it.

Lucy exuded power: sexual power and more. It was clear that she was in control wherever she went. Rachel's admiration was interrupted when she caught wind of the foulest smelling odor. *Ugh, what was that?* The putrid smell seemed to be emanating from Lucy; this Rachel thought impossible. Rachel thanked Lucy and moved quickly to get away from the foul air, and walked along the sidewalk toward the clinic.

The sign in front of the building said, 'AAA Women's Health Center,' *an odd name for an abortion clinic,* Rachel thought. A waist-high chain link fence separated the clinic property from the public sidewalk. Standing on the other side of the fence was the smiling face of a girl who appeared to be about her age.

"Hi there, sweetie!" the girl called out from the sidewalk. "I'm Cari, and I've got some information that will help you." Curiously, she walked over and took the packet of brochures that Cari handed her. "This is a list of free resources that are available to help you and your baby. How far along are you?" Cari asked.

"I'm not sure I'm pregnant," Rachel said, "I'm just here for a test."

"I know a place that can get you a free pregnancy test and an ultrasound if you need it," Cari offered.

"No thanks, I've already got this appointment."

"They're just going to give you the same test you can get with us for free. Why don't you save your money?" Cari said.

As tempting as this offer was, Rachel just wanted to get inside and have the test done, so she was willing to pay the money, although she really couldn't afford it. Rachel then noticed four other people standing along the sidewalk: two girls, a fat older man sporting a graying goatee and dark glasses; he was next to the largest man she had ever seen. The giant had to have been a former linebacker; he was easily over six and a half feet and 350 pounds of solid muscle – incredible. They all kept glancing her way, but she averted her eyes as they recited things from their books. Just then, they started singing, 'Silent Night,' and Rachel thought this was weird. "What're those people doing Christmas caroling in November? Are they some kind of glee club for freaks?" she asked.

"Those people are praying for you and your baby. We're here because we want to help both of you. Jesus loves you both and we're here to show that you don't have to go through this pregnancy by yourself. Even Jesus didn't carry His cross alone, so He doesn't expect you to do it alone either. We want to help you."

"Ok, see ya," Rachel said as she walked toward the clinic. Talking about Jesus was weird, and it made her very uncomfortable. Rachel didn't know much about church; she couldn't remember ever going to church. She got most of her ideas about religion and religious people from TV, and what she saw was not the least bit interesting: images of judgmental, uptight people, telling each other what not to do and giving all their money to the guys with weird hairdos and funky suits. She had to admit that Cari seemed very nice, even if she were some kind of religious freak.

5

Focusing her attention on where she was going, Rachel took note of the pretty purple paint on the brick building and wondered why anyone would ever think of painting brick. It was a creative idea which she noted for future reference. The exterior was squeaky clean; the lawn was well maintained, and everything was neat and orderly. What a contrast to the neighboring slum, filled with recent immigrants, street people wearing tattered clothing, dilapidated buildings, and garbage strewn everywhere. Across the street were a strip mall with a Mexican restaurant, a liquor store, two pawnshops, and a fortuneteller displaying a hand-written sign in the window. Rachel couldn't wait to get inside and away from the heat that burned with urban decay and assaulted her senses. This clinic was definitely an oasis of sorts.

Rachel spent her whole life in Florida. She opened the clinic door and anticipated the refreshing burst of cool air. Instead, what she got was a reception area filled with irritated girls sweating as the overhead fan pushed the hot air around the room. The girls stared listlessly at an old black and white TV showing an afternoon soap opera in which the actors' lives looked more interesting than the group in the clinic.

Rachel walked up to the receptionist behind the glass-enclosed counter. The window slid to the side and the rush of cool air she had anticipated at the door came rushing through, and it mixed with the strong scent of cigarette smoke on the raspy breath of the older lady, who had a too-short hairdo and a big name tag that identified her as 'Laide.' The woman handed Rachel a clipboard and said, "Fill this out, and bring it back to me," before quickly closing the window again.

Somebody's cranky, Rachel thought to herself as she grabbed the clipboard and went to sit down in a vacant chair between two other girls. She felt a little cramped, and despite the noisy, useless fan, Rachel began filling out the questionnaire.

Name ... Address ... Social Security Number ... Known Allergies .... There were some check boxes listed under 'Reason for Visit' and Rachel chose 'Pregnancy Test' but noted the other two options were 'Birth Control Consultation' and 'Termination.' While she filled out the rest of the form, a door opened and a rush of cooler air blew out into the waiting area.

6

"Yolanda?" called out a lady wearing blue scrubs and a white lab coat. A large, African American girl to Rachel's right got up quickly.

"Right here," she said, and followed the lady into the back office area. When Rachel got to the 'Emergency Contact Name and Number,' she wrote down Tom's information. Then signed the consent part and the HIPPA paperwork and brought it back to the receptionist.

"That will be $50 cash," the smoky-smelling, shorthaired lady said dryly as she collected the fee from Rachel. Glancing at her name on the clipboard, she added, "You're late."

"Yes, I am. That's why I am here," said Rachel with an expectant grin and a roll of her eyes, but the attempt at humor went right over the woman's head – or she just wasn't in the mood.

"Have a seat until your name is called." The receptionist said stonily.

Returning to her seat, Rachel tried to distract herself with the TV, but she found that she just couldn't get into watching some woman accusing her husband of sleeping with another woman. *How can people watch this stuff?* she wondered. Giving up on the TV, Rachel picked up the lone magazine on the coffee table, and to her disgust found that it was 'Golf Digest.' Thwarted in her efforts at distraction, Rachel just blocked out the world around her, closed her eyes, and tried to relax … Yeah … just tuning it out … letting it go … ZZZZZZZZZZZ

Chapter 2

TIME: "Not-Now"

"PUSH! C'mon Honey. PUSH!" Tom yelled.

AAAAHHHHH! was the only sound that came from Rachel as she pushed one more time and heard her newborn baby's cry.

"Congratulations, Rachel! Your daughter is beautiful," Doctor Aledo said as she pulled the newborn free and watched Tom carefully cut the umbilical cord. The sound of her baby's cry broke all the tension in Rachel's body as she let go with a flood of hormone-induced emotions.

"Let me hold her," Rachel sobbed.

She had a daughter, whom she knew was coming thanks to the ultrasound technician at the Crisis Pregnancy Center. Rachel had seen the beautiful 4-D ultrasound image taken at a Church-run clinic that was free of charge. Rachel couldn't believe all that she had been through in the last seven months to get to this point. Cari had been instrumental in this decision by taking her to the appointments and by guiding her throughout the pregnancy. Moreover, when the labor began, Cari was there to help until Tom arrived.

During the pregnancy, Rachel had managed to take some extra online classes. She was almost a semester ahead of where she would have been otherwise. She was less than two years away from her degree but planned to take a semester off to take care of her newborn daughter. With assistance from a woman's advocacy center at her school, Rachel finished her class work and took her exams two weeks early so she could concentrate on the baby's delivery without stressing over her finals. Most of the professors had been helpful and understanding, especially when the advocacy center worked on Rachel's behalf. All but one professor accommodated Rachel's schedule since she was a decent student and was determined to finish her degree. The one professor who offered no sympathy for Rachel's situation, only agreed to give her an incomplete until she took his final exam on his terms.

Tom had completed his degree and had found a job as a junior engineer in a company just outside of town. He now made enough money to get an apartment and lease a new mini van, which he and Rachel would need. They had gotten married the month before, and although Tom's parents demonstrated their disapproval of both Rachel and the situation by boycotting the wedding, Rachel's parents were very supportive.

Rachel silently prayed to God. *Father, thank You for everything, especially for Cari who introduced me to You.* Praying and going to church, though still relatively new to Rachel, had become a comfort. Her seemingly dire situation broke down her mental barriers and allowed her to open up to God and to introduce herself to Him. This started with Cari's friendship and encouragement and continued with her new Church friends through an intimate introduction in prayer. Rachel found herself praying quite a bit lately, mostly prayers of faith and thanksgiving for God's blessings. She came to understand His love and the sacrifice His son Jesus gave when He died for her sins. She believed that His death took away the pain and guilt that her actions merited. Sometimes Rachel felt like she could actually feel God's presence as she communed with Him in prayer, but right now her emotions were overwhelming and went beyond thought or description.

"You did good, babe! She's gorgeous and perfect just like you!" Tom crooned. Tom had been a big surprise to Rachel. The pregnancy had changed him – as if some kind of light switch had gone on and all of a sudden, he was more of a man than the wimpy guy with whom she slept just for fun. Tom had shocked her with his positive response when she had informed him of their situation; he got excited and was totally behind the pregnancy. For him, it meant that the timetable for marrying Rachel had accelerated, and he made all the plans. Knowing that his family would be devastated and blame Rachel, Tom took all the heat from them when he and Rachel told them about the baby. When Tom's parents cut him off financially, Tom acted responsibly and decisively and made it clear that Rachel and their unborn child would have everything they needed no matter what. In the final analysis, he proved himself to Rachel.

9

When it came to God, it was taking Tom a little longer to accept the concept since his analytical mind found it difficult to understand faith. Tom let Rachel lead him in prayer, and he didn't complain about going to Church because it always put Rachel in a good mood when he went with her. And why wouldn't he do something that made her happy, if all it cost him was a little time? While he didn't quite believe, he saw major changes in Rachel's attitude toward him – positive changes that he liked since she started going to church, and he liked it.

"Wow, Rachel, she's so beautiful! I'm jealous! I want a little girl too!" Cari chimed in. Cari and Rachel had really connected, and over the last seven months, Cari had become one of the most important people in her life. In addition to being a volunteer sidewalk counselor, Cari was part of a network of 'Gabriel Angels' who befriended and mentored girls who found themselves in crisis pregnancy situations. Although Cari was a few years older than Rachel, the two really hit it off, and found, that they had a lot of similarities in the things they liked and disliked, and their personal chemistry was great. Cari was married with two small boys of her own, so she couldn't get together with Rachel as often as she would have liked, but Rachel understood and accepted these limitations; she was thankful for Cari's attention when she could get it. At the beginning of Rachel's pregnancy, Cari had introduced Rachel to her friend Sara who was a student at the same University that Rachel was attending. Sara had been a great help to her as well, making sure that she got to Church and to pre-natal visits and introducing her to more 'Church friends.'

During Rachel's pregnancy, Cari, Sara, and their friends had become Rachel's support network. They cried with her, joked with her, encouraged her, and helped her to get access to government and charitable programs that provided for different needs. They helped her understand that she was not alone, that there were people who cared both for her and her baby and who were willing to help.

Chapter 3

TIME: "Now"

"Chamequa!" the lady in the blue scrubs blurted out from the opened door.

"Right here," a teenage voice chirped in reply. Startled out of her catnap, Rachel opened her eyes just in time to see another young African American girl sashay up to the open door. Looking around the room, Rachel thought it was odd that she was the only "Anglo" there. Rachel was not used to being in places where she was a minority and wondered if the strangeness of it was similar to what black people felt in a majority white population.

Rachel didn't realize how tired she was, and it was kind of stuffy in here – that musty smell was starting to dissipate, or maybe she was just getting used to it and didn't notice it as much. Closing her eyes again, she focused on her breathing.

Chapter 4

TIME: "Not-Now"

"Rita Isabelle Pierce, I baptize you in the name of the Father, the Son, and of the Holy Spirit," the deacon said as he poured water over little Rita's head.

The baby screamed as not-so-muffled laughter went up from the assembly of family and friends. Rita was two months old now and not quite at the stage where she could sleep through the night. Since Tom was the sole breadwinner and needed to be up for work in the morning, most of Rachel's nights were split between sleeping, rocking, and feeding. Rachel was following the instructions of a nursing specialist from the La Leche League, who had told her, among other things, to feed the baby when she was hungry. This also had the secondary effect of preventing Rachel from ovulating. The nurse had said this was a type of normal pattern that nature had built into her to help space births. So far so good. Rachel also learned that this could work up to two full years and beyond, but she didn't see herself breast feeding for that long. For now, though, it just gave the newlyweds one less thing to be concerned about.

As the Rite of Baptism concluded, Rachel looked around at the smiling faces of the people in attendance who were there to help bask in their joy. *This is what it's all about,* she thought, *being around people who love you and don't judge you for the mistakes you've made. This is Christianity – thank You, Jesus, for finding me when You did and bringing me and little Rita into Your family. I pray that You will do the same for Tom when you think that he is ready.*

Cari, Rita's godmother, was beaming as she held her. Rachel pondered the significance of Cari. In some ways she was as much Rita's mother as Rachel. It could truthfully be said that without her, Rita would not be alive. The decision Rachel made to bring Rita's pregnancy to term was in large measure influenced by Cari's demonstration to her that not only could she do it, but that she did not have to go through it by herself. Everything Cari had promised her when they were out in front of

12

the abortion clinic that Saturday last year had come to pass – and more! As a recent convert to Christ, Rachel realized that she had made a mistake by being sexually active before marriage. While she couldn't undo the effects of her mistakes, she had come to realize that the God who loved her enough to sacrifice His own Son for her could still bring about good things in spite of her actions. She was glad not to be on the artificial hormones of the birth control pills. She had actually found herself losing not just baby weight after the birth but, by not being on any chemical contraception, she had also easily lost extra weight that she had been carrying, and now weighed eight pounds less than before she got pregnant!

Rita was an amazing baby. Rachel was certain that sometimes when she was rocking her and humming a lullaby, Rita was trying to hum along. So far, no one else had heard the baby do this, so Rachel not having any proof, didn't want anyone to think she was nuts or bragging the way some new mothers did. Tom did not sing – EVER – so he would not be able to corroborate her story.

Unbeknownst to Rachel, Tom did suspect that there was something special, or at least unique, about his child. Although he never sang to her, it did seem to him that sometimes when he was talking to Rita, that she would fix her eyes on him in a special way that seemed like she was actually hearing him, or at least paying attention to him in a way he had never seen a baby do. But then again, as the youngest child in his family, he had never spent much time with small children, and almost none with babies, so he couldn't really be sure. The last thing that this logical, mechanically oriented man would have done would be to voice such an unusual idea.

Rachel's mother Ruth was beaming too. She didn't get Rachel's new religion thing. She liked Tom, though, and she saw something in him that she wished she had found twenty-one years earlier when she went through her own crisis pregnancy. That situation's results had sent her life down a path of hurt and shame and led to a series of bad relationships and bad decisions. At this moment, though, she was all Grandma – or 'Granny' as she liked to refer to herself. Her first reaction, when

13

she learned of Rachel's pregnancy, had been incredulity, since she had gone to such great lengths to make sure she never got pregnant. She had been disappointed with Rachel because Rachel was the first person in their family to go to college, and she wanted her daughter to finish her degree. That had to be put aside to focus on being a mother, but Tom's loving reaction to Rachel's news and decision to step up and be a man had filled Ruth with pride and joy. She believed them when they said that Rachel would go back and finish her degree. Ruth didn't just like Tom she LOVED him. He was the son she always wanted, and he could do no wrong. He was smart, responsible, and he loved her daughter and granddaughter, and now he had a college degree and a job. What more could a mother want?

"Okay, godmother, that's enough!" Ruth said. "It's Granny's turn to hold the precious baby, yes it is! She wants her Granny doesn't she?" She said it in the goo-goo language that people use around babies and gently but firmly she snatched her grandchild from Cari. Although it was phrased as a question, it was not a request. "I swear this child understands me," exclaimed Ruth. "See how her eyes look at me when I'm talking. I have never seen anything like it before."

"Let me see," Rachel's next oldest sister, Maggie, said. "Wow, look at that! She's looking at me now – it's like she knows what's going on!"

Chapter 5

TIME: "Now"

"Moesha!" the lady with the scrubs called out once again, as she startled Rachel out of the mesmerizing haze.
Was I asleep again? She wondered. A quick glance at her cell phone showed that she had been in the waiting room for close to an hour. *This sucks,* she thought. *But I just have to get this taken care of today.* She stood up and peered through the blinds, and noticed that Cari and her weirdo chorale were still out there doing their thing. Rachel chuckled as she thought that might be a good name for an alternative band. *Cari and the Weirdo Chorale*, Rachel mused while basking in her own wit.

Cari looked like she was talking to another girl, and the conversation was animated, with lots of motions and gestures, although Rachel could not hear what was actually being said. When the girl turned toward the clinic, Rachel saw that it was Yolanda, the first girl who had gone in for her appointment. Yolanda looked like she was crying, and then to Rachel's surprise, Yolanda nodded her head affirmatively to whatever Cari was saying, walked around the fence, and got in a big group hug with her and all her weird choir. *Well it looks like they're happy,* Rachel thought. *Good for them, whatever.*

Turning away from the window, Rachel walked over to a soda machine in the corner. It was lit up, but she didn't hear the usual hum coming from the machine that she would have expected to hear. The sign on the machine read, *$2.00 any combination of bills and coins.* Reaching into her purse, she took out her last two bills to feed into the machine. Surprisingly, the bills went in easily without having to be re-folded or turned around. Rachel pushed the button and heard a familiar *thunk! thunk!,* and like Pavlov's dog, she reached down to get her reward, only to find that the can was warm. She was now the proud owner of a $2 can of warm diet cola, and Rachel now knew why there was no hum – the machine's refrigeration wasn't working. She went over to the tough lady in the window and asked sweetly, "Excuse me do you have any ice?"

"Nope," said the window grouch, quickly sliding the window closed so that none of the precious cool air could get out into the waiting area.

"This place sucks," Rachel muttered and turned around to reclaim her seat. *That crab is either PMS-ing or from New York,* she thought to herself.

"They're all this way, honey," said the thirty-something gal in the power suit. "They're just all about the money. Every time I've come here or have gone anywhere else, it's always the same. I'm Sandy," she said, introducing herself. "You look like this is your first time?"

"Yes, it is," Rachel replied, thankful for a distraction from the monotony and discomfort of the waiting room.

"This is my third time here and fifth time overall," Sandy said very matter-of-factly. "You'd think they'd at least try to treat the paying customers a little better, but most of these workers in here can barely read, much less smile. It's that way in all the abortion clinics. A friend of mine used to do the books in one of these places, and you would not believe the stories she told me. She ended up quitting because of all the shenanigans. She said she was always afraid that they were doing things illegally, and she didn't want to go to jail."

"Really? Were they cooking the books? This seems to be an all-cash business. It would probably be hard to prove they weren't," Rachel said. Having taken a couple of business classes, she felt very in-tune with accounting practices.

"Maybe so; but I don't even want to let you know what she told me about what goes on in there," the woman said. "It might spoil your appetite if I did!"

"What do you mean?" asked Rachel.

"You know how you go to a restaurant and you think its good, then somebody you know ends up working there and telling

16

stories about what the cooks and waiters do to the food, and then you don't want to eat there? Well, you look like you're probably going to need a procedure, and I don't want to tell you what I heard they do, or you might not get done what needs to get done," she said, laughing. "Trust me, honey, you DON'T want to know. Say, you got one of those brochures in your hand that those anti-choice wackos were passing out outside, right? Why don't you give that to me?" She reached for the pamphlets that Rachel had sticking out of her purse. Rachel handed them over without a second thought.

"You don't need to be reading this propaganda either. You need to make up your OWN mind to have an abortion, and let me tell you, when you do, you'll know that it's your OWN decision to control your OWN body YOUR way. So you just have that abortion if you're pregnant," Sandy ordered. She was so into what she was saying that Rachel wondered if the woman realized the irony of the situation – that in fact, she was telling Rachel what to do. It was Sandy's choice and not necessarily Rachel's that she was pushing – *Funny, but no matter*, Rachel thought, *her intentions were pure.*

Sandy then proceeded to recount her life experiences to her, but Rachel was now in a conversation mode where she was only partly listening to what Sandy was saying. She was nodding her head and saying yep and uh-huh to make it seem like she was listening. In reality, her thoughts were elsewhere.

Chapter 6

TIME: "Not-Now"

"I've never seen that before. I've read about a case or two, but I've never actually seen anything like it!" the new doctor explained excitedly to Rita's parents, who by now were quite used to hearing it. "I'd like to run a couple more tests ... with your permission of course," he fumbled expectantly.

"Actually, Doc, I think she's had enough for now," Tom responded. "She's been in there for an hour and needs some fresh air."

"Yes, yes of course, what child wouldn't? We can finish this another time."

Tom didn't have the heart to tell the researcher that he had no intention of bringing his daughter back to the University research center any time soon. Rita was an exceptional five-year-old who was writing music and doing algebra when other kids her age were learning their ABC's...

All the research scientists wanted to study Rita. It started innocently enough when as a small child, without a fully formed palate, she was able to repeat melodies that her mother had sung to her. There were no words at first, at least none that could be understood as words, but the tone and the pitch and the key was unmistakable. Rita was repeating the sounds as she heard them and without missing a beat. For the last five years, she went through numerous physical and intellectual tests at the University. The doctors were always so anxious to examine her with electrodes, MRI's, and other medical procedures, and now it was time to take a break from all of it.

When the Pierces had previously tried to back out of the experiments, the University offered Rachel a staff position with full benefits. She was now a research administrative assistant with the Plant Sciences Department, which was also under the same administration as the Child Development and Psychology Department. This gave the doctors access to Rita on a fairly regular basis, and for Rachel it was cheaper than daycare. Rachel's benefits included free tuition, so she used the opportunity to finish her undergraduate degree in Psychology and her Master's degree in Library Science. Her daughter had put her through school, and now it was time to work in her chosen field of study.

Rita liked most of the tests particularly the ones that challenged her. Although the exams seemed like a game to the little girl, her parents insisted that one of them be present during the testing so that some overzealous researcher never conveniently forgot the rules that were in place when examining their child.

Tom had done pretty well with his job. Each year he had gotten solid performance appraisals and small raises that allowed them to buy a small house and keep up with the payments for their two vehicles.

Rachel never went back to artificial contraception after she finished ecological breast-feeding with Rita. She liked the way she felt, and the same people who taught her about its benefits trained her in the Creighton Model of Natural Family Planning. Rachel found it empowering to be in control of her own fertility and in control of her own body. Each morning she monitored her body's signs, and Tom faithfully recorded the results. In this way, they both knew at all times which days she was fertile and which days she wasn't, and planned their romantic encounters accordingly.

When Rachel had first gone on contraception as a teenager, she had liked that it made her cycles regular. Even though she was no longer regular, she knew when her cycle would start just by the way her body changed. She no longer felt habitually bloated and irritable, and she was now several pounds lighter than when she had first gotten pregnant – the benefits of not putting artificial hormones in her body.

Lately, they had started talking seriously about another child but so far, that's as far as it had gotten – just talk. That was one of the best aspects of their relationship in Rachel's way of thinking, as they communicated about everything and had very few

19

misunderstandings. Every morning they talked about their fertility cycle, and that led them to talk about everything else. Rachel reveled in it. Many of her girlfriends had such poor communication with the men in their lives that they envied her relationship with Tom. The Pierce's routine was pretty consistent: wake up, check and log fertility signs, discuss implications on love life, and/or take appropriate actions, say some quick prayers (always led by Rachel – Tom still wasn't all the way there with faith), shower, and get Rita ready, make bag lunches, and go about the day's affairs. Weekends found them getting together with friends at church for coffee and donuts in the social hall and sometimes making plans for the balance of the day. Life was agreeable. God was good. They were content – one might even say happy.

Chapter 7

TIME: "Now"

"Fantasia," the woman in the lab coat yelled out from the half-opened door, and called again, "Fantasia, are you here ...?" No response. "Laide, we got another walk-out," she yelled to the grouchy countenance behind the reception window.

"Whatever! So take the next name on the list!" Laide growled with an annoying nasal whine in her voice.

"Okay, that would be ... Charmain!" she called out as another young pear-shaped girl wearing a halter top that kept having to be pulled down got up to follow her into the back.

"Ha! Walkouts! That happens all the time!" Sandy told Rachel.

"Well if that's the case, why don't they start treating the women better?" Rachel asked.

"Look around this room, honey. Does it look like they need to do anything to attract more business?" Sandy asked. Rachel had to admit that whatever they were doing for marketing must be working, because the place was full. She just wished they would hurry up. She had been here for almost two hours.

"They must do a lot of advertising," Rachel said.

"Honey, the only thing they do is advertise in the phone book. Isn't that where you found them?" she asked while Rachel nodded in assent. "That's why they have AAA in the name – so their ad is first in line under 'abortion' or 'pregnancy.'"

"I have to ask you something. If you knew how bad it was here, why did you come back?" Rachel inquired.

"It's like I told you, they're all the same, and I know at least two other places in town that are much worse. This musty smell is

21

tolerable in here but the stench in another place where I have been just makes you sick. When I went for my third trimester abortion, the place had its own crematorium, and the sickly-sweet smelling smoke in that place is just everywhere. What's more, they charged me $2500 cash since I was in my third trimester. You know they charge by the size of the fetus, so it's cheaper when you have it done earlier rather than later.

"My husband and I had decided to keep that one, but then I got a promotion to vice president at my company, and there was no way I was going to pass that up. But now it's different. I'm almost forty, we have our house, our dream cars, (did you see my jaguar outside?), and we are finally ready. We did everything the financial planners and advisors told us, and waited until we were secure and had money set aside for retirement and emergencies and all that. We traveled and saw what we wanted, and now we are finally ready to start a family."

"Wow, it really sounds like you've done everything right. I really envy that," Rachel exclaimed admiringly, she thought about how much sense it all made. Sandy was a role model, someone who was really in charge and knew how to make things happen. "So why are you here today?"

"Same reason as you sweetie, to get a good pregnancy test. I took one at home and failed it, but I've been feeling morning sickness and putting on a little weight, so I want to confirm it. We're finally ready, and one of the drawbacks of waiting has been that I don't seem to get pregnant as easily as I used to. It's been four years since my last procedure, and I've been off of Norplant for a year now – it's just taking me a little longer right now," Sandy explained.

"Gosh, I wish I could trade places with you, Sandy!"

"Are you still in school? Yes? Then you're doing the right thing by coming here. This is one of the few places left that helps women. So many others have closed down over the years, so just look beyond how they treat you to see the real power of the choice that they give you to exercise your right as a woman. Take my advice, when you do get your procedure, pay the extra for the anesthesia – it's worth it. You may feel sick afterwards, but it's better if you're out during the whole thing. Trust me; I've done it both ways. I know what I'm talking about."

Rachel nodded her head at the sagacious wisdom her elder had just imparted. This was a woman she could look up to, and she wanted to be just like her.

Chapter 8

TIME: "Not-Now"

Wanting so much for Rita to have a normal childhood, they had tried regular school but it just wasn't possible. When you're ten years old and can write symphonies and do calculus, there's no way to fit in. The Pierces tried private school, various gifted and talented programs, yet nothing worked. In the end, Rachel began working full time in a library that allowed Rita to spend her day reading at her own pace. This type of hybridized home-schooling worked well for Rita, and with the money Rachel was able to make, they could supplement her education with tutors and grad students who would study with her for an hourly rate.

Rita's IQ was off the chart. The last doctor who tried to put a number on it told them 220, but he admitted that she was so far off the scale that the number was only theoretical and a poor attempt to put a label on something they hadn't really experienced before.

The Pierces lived with the fact that she was an uber-genius, but the thing that really made her special was her tremendous sensitivity to other people. She could look at their faces and quickly analyze their feelings and moods and often seemed to know what they were thinking. Although she was reading expressions and body signs, it did appear to give her a mysterious and uncanny insight that people found very unnerving. She had upset more than one of their friends over the years by revealing that they were hiding something or masking their feelings in a false bravado.

On those occasions, when the ability was a source of inadvertent embarrassment to her parents, Rita would immediately notice and ask, "Did I say the wrong thing again?" Sometimes the innocence and cuteness of this inquiry would completely diffuse the situation, but not always. At times, though, it did remind people that they were dealing with the immaturities of a child who, although brilliant, had very little first hand experience with social finesse.

24

Beyond reading body signs, Rita had a genuine concern for other people's feelings and true empathy for them. She seemed to be able to feel people's pain, or at least to connect with the fact that they were suffering, and she wanted to help them to feel better.

For his part, Tom was dreaming of taking her to a casino when she was old enough to get into high stakes poker tournaments – she was that good.

A recent experience with a sick neighbor led Rita to take an interest in medicine and devour every biology and nursing textbook she could get. This had necessitated a talk about the birds and the bees with her mother, a discussion scheduled for a day when Tom was conveniently working late. In her various readings, Rita had of course come across many age-inappropriate references, so it was not so much a biological discussion as it was a moral one. The textbooks having been written for scientifically-oriented college students who were memorizing facts, were, for the most part, void of any moral context for procreative activities, thus making it necessary for her parents to fill in the ethical blanks.

"Mom, did you know that our lungs inhale over two million liters of air every day?"

"No, honey, I didn't know that." This type of exchange was taking place several times a day, but Rachel never tired of it. Learning was as natural as breathing to Rita, and her mother was just so thankful for her daughter's interest in absorbing information. She was a walking encyclopedia, and her parents were so proud of their little prodigy.

Rachel and Tom's second child, Elijah, was now almost four, and although he was a bright child relative to the general population, he was not Rita. Elijah was very much a typical four-year-old boy. He was enrolled in the early childhood program at their local parish school.

25

Religious education was important to Rachel because she had never had it as a child, so she made sure her kids got the best faith formation she could arrange. Rita had already read most of the Catechism of the Catholic Church without completely understanding the *Life in Christ* section, and had virtually memorized the four Gospels, Genesis, and Exodus.

Young Rita shared her mom's passion for prayer and conscious contact with God. She was also playing a big role in her little brother's religious formation. She was his godmother. Rita enjoyed helping her mother teach religion to the younger kids at Church, and having another kid sharing the classroom instruction responsibilities with an adult made all the kids that much more interested in learning. Tom, while a supportive and loving father and husband, still had his doubts about God, but tried to avoid voicing them out of respect for Rachel and the commitment they had made to raise the children in the faith of the apostles. Lately, his daughter had begun to challenge him on some things and was starting to push the envelope more and more. *Her inquiries were becoming more detailed and personal,* Tom thought as he recalled their last conversation.

"Daddy, how come you don't go to Communion? Did you do something really bad?" she asked teasingly, already knowing the answer because she had heard it so many times before.

"No, honey, I just don't feel like I should go right now."

"But you never go, Daddy. Have you ever received the Body of Christ?" Rita inquired. She had never phrased it quite like this.

"Well, I guess not, honey … it's just not the right time for Daddy yet," Tom responded.

"Why is that?"

"Well, honey there's just some things that I need to work through first. Hey let's go get an ice cream!"

Rita was astute enough to know that the conversation was over; she wasn't going to turn down an ice cream. Tom had nipped it

26

in the bud for now, but he knew it would come up again, and wasn't sure how to handle it.

Chapter 9

TIME: "Now"

Rachel grimaced as the sickening aftertaste of warm aspartame attacked her taste buds. *Nasty!* Rachel said to herself as the hot liquid slid down the back of her throat and seemed to stick there. Not only was the soda hot but so was Rachel – hot, bothered, and restless. Sandy had already been called into the back offices. Now Rachel was sitting there with a new group of women who had made their way into the clinic. A blond teenage girl in a plaid private school uniform sat down next to Rachel. The girl reeked of cigarette smoke, and Rachel held her breath, hoping that she would be called next.

"Is that diet cola from the machine?" the schoolgirl asked pointing at Rachel's now abandoned diet cola can on the coffee table.

"Ya, it is," Rachel nodded. "It's hot soda, which is why I'm not drinking it."

"Thanks for the warning. Guess I'll just wait until later to get a drink," the girl responded. "I'm so nervous I'd probably pee on myself anyway if I drank something right now. Strange how there doesn't seem to be a bathroom out here," the girl continued.

"It's because this whole place sucks," replied Rachel with frustration. She then proceeded to tell the girl about her experience in the waiting room thus far.

"Wow, you're right, this place does suck," the girl said with empathy in her voice. "I'm Catherine, by the way. I came here a few months ago with my mother to get birth control pills, and the woman at the window made me cry with her comments. With her looks, I bet she's weird. It creeps me out the way she looks at me." Catherine said.

"I'm Rachel. So you came here for birth control a few months ago and now you're back. Did you screw up taking the pill?"

28

"Well kinda, sorta …." Catherine said sheepishly. "My mom put me on the pill for my fourteenth birthday last summer. She wanted me to be ready for eighth grade since she knew kids were having sex by then. The problem was, the pill gave me blurred vision, and I hyperventilated like an asthmatic person, so the doctor took me off the pill and hooked me up with a diaphragm. Only thing is, it didn't work too well because now I'm pregnant, and my mom would kill me if she knew."

"You're only fourteen?" Rachel exclaimed in surprise. "You look seventeen, easily."

"I know that's what my boyfriend Stevie thought when I first met him thanks to L'Aurignale cosmetics." Catherine said, giggling. "Funny thing is I thought he was seventeen, but he's actually twenty-five! Not only does he have a driver's license, but he can also buy cigarettes and wine coolers for us. My mom really likes him but we told her that he's seventeen, and it helps that he looks it 'cause she would freak if she knew he was twenty-five. Fortunately, he lives clear across town in his parents' basement and his family doesn't go to church, so there's not much of a chance anyone would say anything. She thinks he's seventeen, and she jokes with him about becoming jail bait next year – if she only knew!"

"Does he still think you're seventeen?"

"No, he knows my real age, but he's so in love with me that it doesn't matter to him. He loves me so much that he made my appointment for me and gave me the $700 cash for my procedure today. And tomorrow he's going to take me shopping and buy me something special, Catherine said excitedly. "He loves me. He had to work to pay for everything. He's an assistant french fry bagger over at Freddy's Fish Fry, and he picked up the extra hours so I could get this procedure. He's working right now because he loves me, and he'd be here if he could."

"So, if your mom doesn't know you're pregnant, and he didn't drive you here, how did you get down here? Did you take a bus?"

29

"I'm so lucky that I go to St. Monica's, and fortunately the nurse at my school, Ms. Judiz is totally cool. She drove me down here and told Pastor Dumas that I was sick with 'girl problems,' so he didn't question her. She's teaches bible study, she's on the school board, and she runs all the fundraising things at the church, so the pastor totally trusts her."

"Ms. Judiz said that I had a right to not be pregnant at my age," Catherine continued. "She said she had done this three times herself, so she knew what I needed. She also told me not to tell anyone or say who had gotten me pregnant because it wasn't anyone's business. She's going to pick me up when I'm done.

"Unfortunately, I was so nervous when I got here that I forgot her advice and told that mean old witch Laide about my boyfriend being twenty-five, and she just put her hands over her ears like a little kid and yelled 'la la la I'm not listening', and told me I better not tell lies like that again or I'd be in trouble. She scares me," Catherine confessed.

Rachel was no lawyer but she knew that a twenty-five-year-old loser sleeping with a fourteen-year-old was against the law. *So maybe that's what Sandy meant,* Rachel thought to herself. She remembered Sandy talking about the illegal activities that go on here, and that the clinic was supposed to report this type of thing to the police. But if they claimed they didn't know Catherine was fourteen and impregnated by a much older adult, then they got to keep the $700 and stay out of trouble. Rachel's thoughts were interrupted by an old man's voice at the main door.

"Good afternoon, Laide" said the old man wearing blue scrubs and a white lab coat. *This must be the doctor,* Rachel thought.

"Oh, Dr. Cutter, let me get the door for you," Laide said as she jumped up and came out from behind the air-conditioned office door to assist the honored physician.

"Laide, you've always taken good care of me," he said, winking as he walked through the door she held. Rachel noticed he had a cane and was limping, favoring his right side that also held a paper bag with two cans of Lysol sticking out as he trudged slowly across the floor. As Laide went to open the office door, the doctor grabbed her backside.

"Oh, doctor," she gasped, jumping slightly as she stifled her humiliation at his inappropriate behavior. Since Dr. Cutter was the only abortionist she could get, she knew her business needed him more than she needed her pride, so she endured his shenanigans. Laide turned and gave everyone in the room a saccharine grin, pretending it was just a playful gesture between consenting friends instead of an unwelcome and inappropriate invasion of her personal space.

In truth, Laide hated Dr. Cutter. He had botched several abortions and cost her some very expensive out-of-court settlements, due both to malpractice suits and inappropriate conduct with patients. He had punctured a girl's uterus one time in the course of a second trimester abortion, resulting in a radical hysterectomy. Another settlement was for molesting a patient who he wrongly thought was too scared to report it.

Cutter was a hack and pervert. Like most abortionists, he had graduated at the bottom of his class; he couldn't qualify for any specialized area, which left him practicing general medicine. Although people think of abortionists as OB/GYN doctors, most legitimate specialists will have nothing to do with abortionists. Even pro-choice doctors consider abortionists pariahs, and isolate them socially because what they do is not considered medicine. It is one thing to be in favor of the philosophical concept of women's freedom of choice, but quite another to actually rip apart living unborn babies.

Although Cutter still had his medical license, he didn't carry malpractice insurance, as no company would touch him. This left Laide with the liability of a lawsuit if he screwed up again. It was a high risk to take, but the bottom line on her bank statement made this a rough partnership. Laide knew Cutter was addicted to prescription drugs and could barely hold a speculum half the time. Three other abortionists in the area had their own practices, so she was stuck with Cutter. The benefit of using

31

Cutter was that he'd write her any prescription she wanted, and Laide took full advantage of this.

Nobody wanted to do abortions anymore. Most of the medical schools were very politically correct and did their best to train doctors to think in a moral vacuum. Despite turning out class after class of secular humanist doctors who were effectively pro-choice, the stigma attached to being an abortionist kept most of these doctors from the field. Those who would commit abortions did so surreptitiously for fear of tarnishing their professional reputations.

Laide had made millions over the years, and run a very tight business with low overhead costs – except for Cutter, but then again, he was the one who provided the profit margin. Laide and her business colleagues had hired professional lobbyists to work for their cause in the state legislature with the intent of making it mandatory for all state medical schools to teach abortion procedures. Because of the amount of money funneled into the coffers of many legislators, this was getting very close to passing during the current legislative session.

The main issue was that, like Cutter, most abortionists were now senior citizens. They were part of a generation that came of age during the sixties and seventies sexual revolution – before ultrasound. Unless the situation changed, within ten years, abortions might be legal, but doctors agreeing to perform the procedure would be extremely scarce. It was this situation that was the weakest link in the abortion service delivery chain.

Laide and her competitors had put their differences aside and given large amounts of money to high-powered lobbyists who were experts at political manipulation. They could outspend the pro-life political forces by a factor of ten thousand. Their organization, the Abortion Sisterhood Society promoted an even more devious scheme, in which they wanted to take the specula out of the hands of doctors and put them into the hands of laymen. If they were successful in getting laws passed where abortions could be performed by people without medical degrees, all their problems would be solved.

Abortions could then be classified as mechanical jobs, where the only diagnostic requirement would be a pregnancy test. Once a woman confirmed she was pregnant, she could go to a place where a state licensed layman who had 'taken some classes' would perform the abortion instead of a certified medical doctor.

Laide, although only a nurse, had performed many illegal abortions over the years when an abortionist was unavailable. She had even trained a couple of her workers to do them as well. Abortions were simple, and once a girl was knocked out from meds, she wouldn't know who had done the procedure anyway.

"Marsha, whose turn is it to see the good doctor?" Laide asked.

"That would be Catherine," the lady in the blue scrubs said, holding the door open for the Catholic school girl.

"That's it. I've had enough! I've been here all day, and now you're taking people in front of me? Sorry Catherine, no offense. I'm out of here," said Rachel, standing up and getting ready to walk out, glancing over at the window where Laide had reassumed her position.

Rachel noticed that Lucy, whom she had met in the parking lot, was in the receptionist area having harsh words with Laide, who seemed to be completely ignoring her. Rachel couldn't hear anything going on behind the glass but she thought she could make out the words, "Don't let Rachel leave!" on Lucy's lips. Lucy caught her eye and smiled at her.

Laide got up, put on her fake grin, and opened the window.

"Rachel, would you come here dear? I'm sorry to keep you waiting. Sharrie will be right back to take you in," she said sweetly. Lucy, standing behind her, winked at Rachel as if to say, "I'm looking out for you." A girl with slightly messy dark hair holding a clipboard met Rachel at the door and ushered her into the back. It was not a huge building, probably no more than 2500 square feet, and it had originally been a house where people raised their children and had Christmas Dinner – once upon a

33

time. Rachel walked down the short hallway to a small room, which looked like it may have been a big closet at one point in the distant past.

"Okay, have a seat right here and let me take your blood pressure," the girl said, gesturing for her to sit on the examination table where a piece of wrinkled tissue paper that had obviously been sat on before awaited her. *Well, after what I've seen so far this shouldn't surprise me,* Rachel thought, thankful that there was at least some air conditioning in this part of the building.

Rachel had assumed the girl was her nurse, but as the girl wrapped the blood pressure monitor on her arm, Rachel read the name 'Sharrie' that was printed on the badge, and the title printed neatly below it was, 'Reproductive Healthcare Associate'. So she wasn't a nurse. Then Rachel remembered what Sandy had told her about the workers in here earlier and thought sarcastically, *that's odd, not only can't they read and write but their parents can't spell either.* Sharrie started inflating the cuff – *puff puff puff puff puff puff puff puff puff puff puff.*

"OWW! Stop that! You're hurting me!" Rachel yelled at Sharrie.

"Ooops sorry, this is only my second day. I guess I did it too hard, right?"

"Whatever gave you that idea?" Rachel said derisively, while rubbing what used to be her left arm. "You just about squeezed off my arm!"

Sharrie knew she had failed again, but she was used to disappointing people. She knew most others were smarter than she was which is why she had dropped out of school at sixteen to smoke pot with her boyfriend and follow an old-style psychedelic rock band. They had lived in a car and when Sharrie became pregnant, her boyfriend took off. After the baby, she hooked up with another loser, got pregnant again, and now lived in government-subsidized housing by herself, having had both children taken away by Child Protective Services several months prior due to neglect.

Part of her 'Personal Life Success Plan' that her social worker had prepared for her after she graduated from a twelve hour 'life-skills' class involved: bathing regularly, brushing her hair and teeth, getting an ID card, cashing her welfare checks, and getting a job. Her worker knew that she didn't like to read, so instead of writing out a check list for her she had cut pictures out of magazines of what Sharrie was supposed to do every day and glued them to a piece of poster board. Then Sharrie put it next to the sofa bed that she slept on every night. So far, she was doing pretty well on her plan. She bathed almost every day, which was better than she used to do, and had started brushing her hair and teeth almost as often, although rarely did she succeed in doing all three things on the same exact day. She had her ID card for the check-cashing store, but had really struggled with finding a job. Even with her hair combed and her teeth brushed the fast food places wouldn't hire her because she couldn't count change back to customers, tell time on an analogue clock or read the menu, for that matter. Lacking basic skills, Sharrie was out of luck until this place hired her.

So far, Sharrie liked the job because she got to wear a uniform that Laide was letting her pay off over time. She also got a pretty badge with her name on it, and a fancy sounding title that made her feel good about herself, although she wasn't ready to admit she couldn't read or pronounce or understand the words.

This was her second day wearing the uniform, and she meant to wash it last night but decided to watch TV instead. Sharrie wondered how many days she could get away without washing it – three, maybe four? She hoped she wouldn't spill anything on it so that she could stretch the days out between washing ....

Sharrie left her apartment at the perfect time of the morning so all the neighbors could see her in her new blue scrubs and know that she was a professional now. "I'm an R.H.A.," she had proudly beamed to anyone and everyone who had seen her. So far, Sharrie was doing a good job of hiding the fact that she didn't understand all of what she was supposed to do. She didn't quite grasp how to use the blood pressure device because she couldn't read the dial on the gauge. Therefore, she had just been writing the same blood pressure down for everyone: 120 over 80. She would mark this on the chart in a very professional manner.

35

This was the number the person who trained her had written down when she had tried to teach her how to use the device and it was the only result she knew. No one had complained, and Laide hadn't mentioned anything so no harm no foul.

"I'm so sorry, can I try that again?" Sharrie said as she gently put the cuff back on Rachel's outstretched arm. Sharrie gently squeezed the hand pump to inflate the cuff. *Puff, puff, puff* it went – Sharrie really liked the puffing noise that it made, but could never remember the number of puffs she was supposed to do, and sometimes got carried away. Trying to count just made her head spin, so she silently hummed the nursery rhyme about Jack and Jill while squeezing the pump. Usually by the time she finished the verse 'Jack fell down and broke his crown,' it was time to stop. "120 over 80," she said very matter-of-factly, writing it down on the clipboard.

"Now I'm going to give you some privacy, so you can go ahead and pee in this cup and put it over there on the table when you're finished," Sharrie said, handing Rachel a plastic cup that had been put in an opened plastic wrapper to make it look sterile. Actually, Laide had her own unofficial recycling program for multiple items that could have gotten her in serious trouble had anyone known. But since abortion clinics were rarely, if ever, inspected, most of their records could be shielded under the guise of privacy. It was highly unlikely that anyone would do anything about it.

Rachel got partially undressed as the door closed, followed the instructions she had been given, placed her sample in the designated location, and waited for whatever came next.

"Are you done already?" Sharrie inquired sweetly as the door crept open.

"Uh huh," Rachel nodded as she watched Sharrie open the wrapper on a pregnancy test, discard it on the same tray, and place the test in the sample. Rachel knew this procedure only too well. She had thought that maybe they would do a blood test, but apparently, that wasn't necessary. Rachel thought it was weird that this girl wasn't wearing any gloves, but that was her problem, not Rachel's. After a minute, Sharrie pulled out the test and looked at Rachel with a sad expression on her face. "Oh, I'm sorry, you are pregnant. I know it's not what you wanted to hear right? Let me go get the counselor to help you," Sharrie said as she left the room, closing the door behind her.

Oh God, it was true, Rachel thought. *I'm frickin knocked up!* she screamed inside. *I'm carrying that schmuck's child! AAHHHGGHHH!* She hated Tom right now. Every part of her body hated him because this was obviously all his fault. No one else had ever knocked her up before, and this was NOT supposed to happen. What the hell was wrong with him! Right now she hated not just Tom, but all men, *curse them,* she thought, as she buried her hands in her face.

A startlingly foul smell hit her senses. Oh God, that was just as bad as … Rachel looked up and saw Lucy's cold, penetrating eyes staring through her. Lucy smiled in a pained expression of sympathy, but her dark hollow eyes showed nothing at all. "Oh, you poor dear," Lucy said. Rachel looked away from those lifeless, terrifying eyes and just listened.

"The associate is going to come and take you to the other room for a chat then you can make your appointment for the procedure, Rachel," Lucy explained. "We both know the timing of this pregnancy is all wrong for you. Gosh, you were doing so well in school, too, weren't you?" Rachel nodded. "You have such a bright future ahead of you Rachel. We can't let anything get in the way of that, now can we?" It was a statement, not a question, and Rachel was just spellbound, numbly drinking in every word Lucy said.

"Uh Uh," Rachel mumbled, shaking her head.

"We both know what needs to be done. Fortunately, you've got a rich boyfriend, right? It wouldn't be fair to burden him with a child, now would it? I mean, it's not like he would have to carry it in his body or anything, but he's looking at 18 years of child support payments and custody fights. Does that make sense to you?" Lucy asked without expecting any answer. "Yeah, me either. You are your own woman, Rachel, and you have a right not to be pregnant. He doesn't seem like the kind who could handle it, right? It might not even be a good idea to tell him. Just get him to give you the money without explaining it to him. Tell him it's a test of his trust in you, and then you can surprise him with the news afterwards if you want. He'll be glad that you took care of it on your own. He's probably got too much on his mind studying for finals – he's a senior right? In Engineering?" Lucy asked.

Rachel was just drinking in Lucy's instructions, feeling as if she knew this all along. It all made sense to Rachel now as she sat on the examination table. Lucy was so smart and so powerful, and Rachel felt lucky to have her help at this critical time. She just wished that the woman would take medicine for whatever it was she had that made her reek like putrid rotten eggs and fish guts. *God, that smell was INHUMAN!* Then it occurred to Rachel, that while Lucy could have seen the books in the back of her car, and the school spirit bumper sticker to figure out that she was in school, Rachel didn't remember saying anything to her about her boyfriend being rich or a senior in engineering, did she? Rachel turned her head at the creak of the door opening, and Sharrie appeared.

"Rachel, come with me to the counselor's office. The ladies room is right on the way if you feel sick," Sharrie said, gagging and covering her nose.

"It wasn't me. It was Lucy!" Rachel protested.

Sharrie didn't even acknowledge Lucy and said, "Whatever, come right this way." Rachel followed Sharrie down another short hallway to a room that was very nicely furnished. It stood in such stark contrast to the rest of the place.

"Just take a seat right there," Sharrie said, pointing at a miniature armchair. It was the kind they keep in model homes to make the rooms look bigger. Opposite the chair was a very large mahogany desk with an impressive high-backed, armed executive swivel chair behind it. Sitting in the little chair, Rachel was thankful for the back support it provided, even if it did seem like an unusual choice of furniture. She was a psych major and had had enough classes to see through the set up of this room.

This must be where they try to convince me of something. I should expect a sales job here.

Chapter 10

TIME: "Not-Now"

"Okay, Rita, go long!" Tom said from the side of their house as he prepared to throw the nerf football to his daughter.

"C'mon, Daddy, throw it!" Rita yelled from across the yard, to which Tom responded with a beautiful spiral pass that came right to her.

"Way to go, baby girl!" Tom said with pride. Not only was his daughter a genius, she could play wide receiver! Rita held the ball aloft in her right hand and did a little victory sprint back.

Unseen by the Pierces, two others were close by. One was a tall, handsome, older man, and the other, who resembled a twisted dwarf with distorted facial features, emitted a repulsive odor.

"Get out of here, Ralph!" the revolting one cried. "Tom is mine by an act of his will – it's HIS CHOICE! You have no jurisdiction here," he exclaimed spitefully.

"Nice to see you too, Asmo. It's been awhile." Ralph laughed in reply.

"I don't like the fact that you're here," Asmo stated defiantly. "That means your Boss is up to something, which always means trouble for me."

"You got that right, old buddy!"

"I'm not your buddy, Ralph," Asmo insisted. "My hands and feet still ache from our last encounter!"

"You ought to work on the attitude, Asmo. Maybe it will make your existence more pleasant. If it's any consolation, I didn't bring my rope this time," Ralph kidded. "I'm sorry; I guess I still like to think of how you were before the war: one of the most amazing dream weavers ever. Easily the best in your whole choir! I still don't know what you and the other third were thinking, joining with the rebellion. It was fated to lose from the very start. Why did you sign on for that? What have you gained besides a few perverted ego trips? I mean, now look at you. You've been consumed by your own lusts, which reflect on the outside what goes on inside you."

"At least I don't work for THE MAN," Asmo jeered derisively.

"No Asmo, no, you don't. But have you looked in the mirror lately? You're none too purdy," he teased. "And look at what they've got you doing, messing around with a little engineering guy. Seems like those you report to are not appreciating your talents. Maybe if you had a change of heart my boss would take you back," Ralph said, trying to offer a sense of hope to his former friend, but they both knew there was no way that was ever going to happen. Asmo had given himself completely over to the other side, and it was a one-way trip for guys like him.

"Oh Ralph, you've got it all wrong! I'm in charge around this place. This is my neighborhood, and you're on my turf now," he said menacingly, even though they both knew he was powerless against Ralph and his kind. "In fact, it's time I gave you a little demonstration of what happens in my dominion. Watch this, Ralph. This one's in honor of your little visit," Asmo cackled.

"Okay Rita, on three: right, left, right, then in the corner. Forty, fifteen, three! hike!" Tom said as he received the nerf ball from his daughter and she ran out to the same location as before. The throw started well, and then the wind pulled it right, just enough to be tantalizingly out of reach for Rita to quickly try to follow and catch it. The ball sailed into the road and Rita followed.

An ancient, beat-up, green colored F-150 with racing stripes slammed on the brakes, but not quickly enough, as the truck hit Rita just as she was reaching for the ball.

"Rita! Oh my God!!!" screamed Tom running over to her.

As Asmo gloated and clapped his hands with delight at what he had wrought, Ralph said calmly, "You've got dibs on Tom for the moment, but never forget, Asmo, Rita belongs to my Boss, and all things work together for good, to them that love God, to them

41

who are called according to His purpose." Asmo winced at
Ralph's words as Ralph pulled out his cell phone and dialed 911.

Chapter 11

TIME: "Now"

"Sharrie, would you come here please?" Dr. Cutter's voice called out from another room where a mechanical drone could be heard that sounded like a vacuum cleaner.

"I'm coming, Doctor," Sharrie said, leaving Rachel alone in the new room.

Rachel looked on the wall and saw some large, impressive looking diplomas with seals. No, not diplomas, but certificates of appreciation from the Abortion Sisterhood Society, Planned Patrimony, the United Nations, the Soogee Come-on Foundation, the March of Nickels, International Amnesty – all different abortion advocacy groups. There was a large bookcase behind the desk filled with old hardcover books. Rachel could not tell what they were about, but interspersed between them were collectable dolls from foreign countries, all very sophisticated looking. This was a powerful woman's office, Rachel thought.

Dr. Cutter closed the door behind Sharrie and asked, "Sharrie, have you seen a D and C abortion yet?"

"No, all the ones I seen so far have been socks-on aspirin-nation," Sharrie replied.

"You mean suction-aspiration," the abortionist corrected. This was a horrible form of abortion where the abortionist must first paralyze the closed cervix and then stretch it open. The cervix is designed to remain closed until the baby is ready to be born, which makes this procedure hard to perform. The patient in question was a young girl who had never been pregnant before so it was going to be extra difficult. Cutter inserted a hollow plastic tube with a knife-like edge on the tip into the uterus. The suction, vastly stronger than a home vacuum cleaner, tore the baby's body into pieces. He then cut the deeply rooted placenta

43

from the inner wall of the uterus. The scraps were sucked out into a bottle. One of the assistants then reconstructed the child's body to ensure that no parts had been left inside. Sharrie didn't like doing this part of the job and couldn't remember what the different pieces were called. Puzzles weren't something she was good at.

"Just to help you understand the different pieces better, I'm going to do this one a little differently," he said gaily. "I'm going to do a Dilation and Curettage or D and C."

"D and C are right next to each other in the alphabet," Sharrie observed proudly, showing off her literary prowess to impress the doctor.

"My, you catch on quick don't you," the abortionist said with feigned admiration. *Laide has really outdone herself with this new hire,* he thought, *and more importantly, she looked like a size D cup, just like he requested.* "Come stand right next to me so you can see better, this is very important." He said, wondering if she was wearing a bra. "Okay, good," he said, positioning himself behind her and 'accidentally' brushing her breasts as he instructed her to look into Charmain's birth canal. "This is going to be very messy. Did Laide give you any gloves? No? Well, you'd better have a pair. Why don't you turn those other ones I was wearing over there inside out, I don't see any blood on them," he said indicating a used pair of gloves partially turned inside out already from use.

"I start out by stretching out the cervix, just like the other procedure, except instead of vacuuming it out," he said, powering down the vacuum and putting it aside, "I'm going to insert a curette. See this loop-shaped steel knife? With this I cut the placenta and the fetus into pieces and scrape them out into that basin so that you can see all the pieces and practice putting them back together. Okay? There's going to be a lot of blood with this kind, so get ready … "

About ten minutes later, the abortionist stood up, walked over to the door, opened it, and called out, "Code pink, Laide!" This was the signal that he may have scraped too hard and damaged the uterus, but not enough to require hospitalization. They could cover up the mistake easily enough as long as it was minor, which they've done many times in the past.

"I scraped too hard," Cutter said as Laide entered the room. He pointed at the end of the curette so she could see the pink substance on the end that shouldn't have been there. "I weakened the uterine wall someplace with too much pressure."

"Cutter, you're a butcher!" Laide exclaimed through her clenched teeth as she looked at the young girl on the table. "Let me take a look." As Laide was examining the girl, she wondered what she was going to do since she could no longer trust Cutter to perform even the simplest procedures.

"Well, the good news is she'll probably be okay in the short term, but will endure a few days of pain," Laide said as she exhaled, knowing that she just barely missed being sued again. "When she's awake, I'll explain the discomfort as something normal, give her some pain pills, and have her sign a post-op disclaimer."

This girl was young – maybe no more than fifteen or sixteen on the outside, one of the younger ones he had worked on recently. These days he was seeing less and less younger girls as more of them seemed to be putting off becoming sexually active until later. And if they did get pregnant, larger percentages were opting to keep their babies due to better support from their families. Girls rarely submitted to abortions when they felt secure in their family's support for their pregnancy.

The old stigma attached to being pregnant out of wedlock was almost an anachronism. On rare occasions, they would get the occasional preacher's daughter or professional parents forcing their daughter or son's girlfriend to abort to save their precious reputations. He was seeing college girls and career women proportionately more than he could ever remember. Yes, Cutter had noticed a significant demographic shift in the customer base over the last ten years or so.

Cutter looked at the girl's chart and saw that a girlfriend had brought her in. *Good*, he thought, *it means that there's a 90% chance her family doesn't know about this. Laide has enough pain medication to get the girl through the week of discomfort, after which time her pain will subside. The scar tissue left behind may prevent her from having children in the future, but by that time, I will be dead. The girl probably won't even make the connection between the infertility and the abortion.*

Cutter knew that women who suffered abortions at an early age tended to block out the memory over time and rarely discus what happened with their real doctors.

"I've got some extra Percocet samples I can give her," Laide said.

Cutter smiled at the way Laide dispensed medication. They both knew that drug companies did not give away samples of narcotics like they do for medications like Viagra. This came from Laide's personal stash. Percocet was the best medication to give, since one of the side effects is stomach pain. Laide, who had an ample supply of the pills thanks to Cutter's open-ended prescription, dispensed this medication like M&M's to the girls he messed up on and didn't warn them not to take it on an empty stomach.

As he exited the room Laide's long-time assistant, Mona, came in wearing gloves, and picked up the specula and a bin filled with baby parts. She turned and said to Sharrie, "C'mon, girl, let me show you how we make sure the doctor got it all. Do you like puzzles? No, of course you wouldn't. Never mind, this is just something you need to learn, come back to the kitchen with me."

The kitchen was an area in the building that actually used to be a kitchen when the building was somebody's home. It had a couple of old refrigerators, one where the employees could keep their bag lunches. They were required to eat outdoors at the picnic table in the back yard. The other refrigerator was used to store the dead baby parts. Laide had a contract with the local university medical center where, for a nominal fee, she would provide them with a large supply of fetal tissue to experiment on. She also contracted with a cosmetic company that sent a truck twice a week to pick up the bodies that the university didn't want. L'Aurignale Cosmetics used the fetuses as a key ingredient in several beauty powders and creams that would be listed on the label as collagen.

46

"Good afternoon, I'm Doctor Cutter, and I'll be taking care of you today," he said sweetly to the girl lying on the table with her legs spread and held in place by stirrups. *Wow, this one is really young, couldn't be in high school yet,* he thought. Catherine had washed her face and removed all her make up before the abortionist came in, and she looked her age for the first time since getting up this morning. *This one was perfect.* "Sharrie, would you give me a moment or two with the patient? It's time for your cigarette break, I think, and do close the door behind you dear." Cutter loved this job!

Chapter 12

TIME: "Now"

Finally, a sharp looking woman in her early forties strode into the room, closing the door behind her as she walked over and shook Rachel's hand before taking her place behind the desk. She was wearing a dark blue power suit with shoulder pads, and her long brown hair was poofed up eighties style, but it looked good. She accessorized well, and the overall effect was clean. Her make up was perfect, just enough that men might not be able to tell that she was wearing any – but of course, any woman could clearly see otherwise.

"Hi, Rachel, I'm Candy. Sorry about making you wait. I don't like to do that, but as you can see, we're very busy around here," she said in a half-hearted attempt to appear apologetic.

"Ok, so how does this counseling work?" Rachel replied

"Well, Rachel, I've got your pregnancy test results here, and it's time to decide what to do," Candy said without making eye contact.

Candy was exceptionally perceptive; she had been in sales since she was a kid working in her father's hardware store. The family's business had closed in the early 1980's after almost 100 years and four generations working for the store. With the arrival of the ubiquitous chain hardware outlets, which put many smaller family-run stores out of business, her father suffered a stroke and passed away. His prolonged convalescence had wiped out the family savings and left Candy and her mother deeply in debt. Candy had to quit college, and come home to help her mother make ends meet. She had been raised in a strong family where women's opinions about business matters were always given a fair hearing, and at the small Catholic college she attended, Candy had fallen in love with the principles of radical feminism.

Many of her professors belonged to such groups as the National Organization for Women, Women Against Men, and Catholics for a Free Choice. Some of her professors, who belonged to a religious order, 'Order of Our Lady's Handmaidens,' paid no heed to any church authorities or teachings, and had instilled in her a deep-seated sense of victim hood for having been born a woman in a world where women were dominated by men. They had taught her to despise and resent the religion she had grown up with, and to see all women as subjects of oppression in need of self-liberation. Candy had listened and studied with relish, and although a couple of professors had tried to turn her on to the merits of goddess worship, in the end, she preferred agnosticism to praying.

Some of the women professors did not seek equality with men, but rather sought an expression of the female person that was independent of men altogether. Often, they spelled the word 'Women' as 'Womyn' or even 'Wymyn' because to keep the original spelling would have been to allow them to be defined by a relationship to men, which was unacceptable. Gender independence, rather than interdependence, was seen as the ultimate expression of womanhood. The only time they ever talked about equality was as it related to sexual issues. Men and women were fundamentally different in that men could have sex and not get pregnant; the only way to equal the playing field was to assure that women could have sex and not get pregnant, or, if they did get pregnant, that they were not expected to carry the child to term.

When Candy withdrew from school, one of her professors, Sister Sophia (self-named after the Greek goddess of wisdom rather than a Catholic saint), had made a few calls on her behalf and gotten her a job at Planned Patrimony selling abortions over the telephone. Candy was an exceptional salesperson and went from salesperson to sales manager, then director in just a few short years. Later, she got an offer from the owner of a large chain of abortion clinics, and she began really making the money. Candy made a very good living in the abortion business, but things started to change with malpractice lawsuits, mismanagement, and a dwindling, aging pool of abortionists. Soon many of the businesses closed up shop, so Candy had taken a job with Laide, whom she'd met during her prior employment.

49

Candy considered Laide a lesbian pill popper whom she despised, but the money was very good. She had worked for lesbians before at the college. Many of her teachers had been out of the closet, and she was okay with that. What Candy didn't like about Laide was the erratic behavior and the cheapness of the woman that seemed exacerbated by the drugs she took. Laide cut many corners, many of which were illegal, but one of the benefits of hiring really ignorant people was that they did not know their rights as employees. Most of the people Laide hired couldn't find a job in the mainstream and didn't complain about the unsanitary conditions, being asked to touch sharp, bloody things, recycle certain items without proper sterilization, or other unsafe practices. Few of them had ever heard of OSHA, and none of them knew what it stood for or could spell it. They were just happy to have a job.

Laide had chosen to go into the most unregulated business in America. Where once abortionists had to ply their trade in the back alleys of America, they now were able to do it legally. Yet many of the same people who used to do it illegally were using the same techniques with the same mechanical limitations as before – but now the law favored them. Because this activity was all wrapped up in the issue of privacy, the clinics were almost never inspected or monitored, and their victims rarely complained of mistreatment, malpractice, or anything else because of the embarrassment and shame associated with their abortion or the activities that led up to it.

Candy had done well over the years, winning numerous sales awards and industry recognitions. She was under no illusions about what she did. At conventions, she used to brag to her colleagues that you could populate a small country with all the fetuses she had eliminated. One of her former employees at Planned Patrimony even proposed the name 'Candyland' for this hypothetical country. Another of her old colleagues from her telephone sales days had mounted a toy toilette that made a mechanical flushing sound on a wooden platform, and had it engraved, 'another one goes to Candyland.' Someone in the office would flush it whenever a sale was made by phone. Business had been so good that they quit replacing the batteries on it after a couple of months, selling abortions to girls who didn't want to be pregnant was like shooting fish in a barrel; even the least professional salesperson could do it and make good money at it.

Candy could read people exceptionally well. She had attended every kind of sales and negotiation training over the years, and it took her only a moment to get an accurate read on the situation. In front of her was a girl who was frustrated with her treatment since walking into the assembly-line atmosphere of this abortion clinic. Candy was going to have to play down her treatment and focus on stoking the coals of panic that were undoubtedly there as well. Less frustration, more fear, uncertainly, and doubt – that was how this needed to play out.

"Rachel, believe it or not, I know how you feel right now." Candy said with pure innocence. This was a lie – Candy had never been pregnant. "I remember how scared I was when I was 21 and had no one to help me raise a kid, and I'd have had to quit school early. I feel very sorry for you; I mean, seriously, how would you raise a kid when you're really just a kid yourself? What will your parents think if they find out you're pregnant? Will they be proud? Will they be happy?"

These were seeder questions she was planting in Rachel's mind to overwhelm her. Now she would build on the fears and make her feel inadequate. "I know you have a lot to think about, but I want to kind of help you to understand the reality of your situation. So, Rachel, are you on a full scholarship? No? Do you live at home? Yes. Wow. So your parents … are you going to ask them to raise your child while they're paying for your school? How much will it cost to have the baby? Do you have your own insurance? Do you have a steady job? How will you get a place of your own, and who will babysit the kid while you are out working? Where will you buy clothing for a child? What about visitation rights for the father? Will he pay child support? Will it be enough? Suppose your new boyfriends don't get along with him? Have you thought about the possible drama? Do you have a good lawyer? Where will they go to school?" Candy bombarded Rachel with question after question.

51

Rachel's head was spinning as she was shaking it yes to one question, no to the next, yes to one, no to another. The whole time Candy was guiding the conversation. "So, Rachel," Candy said for emphasis, while slightly leaning forward in her chair, "are you really ready to have a baby at this time?" This was a trial close question Candy has posed to get Rachel's agreement in principle. Now she slowly moved back in her chair and said nothing as she waited for Rachel to say the next thing.

"Ah, Ah ... ," Rachel stammered, "I don't think I am, no, but ... I don't know it's just all so much to think about. I need to get my thoughts straight ...." Candy had her right where she wanted her.

"Rachel, I know how you feel right now. It's overwhelming. I, and many other women, have felt the same way at one time or another in our lives and we've found that sometimes it really helps to put things down on paper to sort through things logically rather than emotionally. That makes sense, doesn't it?" Candy asked, and Rachel nodded her head yes, because that made perfect sense to her. "You've taken history class, right? You've heard of Ben Franklin, I imagine?" Candy continued. Now it was time to close the deal using one of the oldest sales tactics in the business: the Ben Franklin close.

"They say that Ben Franklin was one of the wisest people who ever lived. Old Ben used to make big decisions by splitting a piece of paper in half and writing all the reasons why he should do something on one side, and all the reasons he shouldn't on the other. Once that was done, he'd count them up, and the side that had the most reasons was what he went with. He thought that putting it down on paper helped to take the emotion out of the decision and make the best answer more obvious. Does that sound logical to you?" Candy asked.

Rachel nodded yes. It sounded very smart to her indeed. "Ok, then, so let's try it," said Candy, handing her a pre-folded piece of paper. "You have two columns. On the top of the left column put 'not now,' and on the top of the right column put 'motherhood now.'" Rachel did as instructed and waited for further directions. "Now, Rachel, let's just think things through, starting with the 'not now' column. Do you have a full-time job? No? Okay, put that down. Do you want to have to marry the father? No? Okay, put that down. Do you have a place of your own? No? Put that down. Do you have a nice car? No? Have you finished your degree yet? No. Put that down."

Candy continued to sow seeds of doubt until not only one side of the paper was full but the backside of that column as well. Then she said, "Okay, that's enough for now. Let's look at the other side of the paper to be fair. What good reasons can you think of to have a baby right now?" This was an open-ended question, and Candy provided no ready-made, set-up questions. Silence.

"Well, babies are cute," Rachel admitted meekly.

"So are puppies, but, okay, put that down. What other reason is there to become a mother right now?" Again, silence. Candy let the silence grow, knowing what the outcome would have to be in Rachel's head. The silence was past being uncomfortable and was now unbearable.

"Well, I guess that's it," Rachel said.

"Rachel, when you look in the left-hand column, how many reasons do you see?" Candy asked while Rachel counted.

"Thirty."

"Now, how many do you have on the other side?

"One."

Candy said nothing else for a moment and let the results of the exercise sink into Rachel's consciousness. Then she opened her appointment book and looked at Rachel's chart. "So it's been six weeks since your last cycle? The fetus is probably too small to extract just yet it's just a mass of cells really – think of it as a cancer that needs to be removed, except it's a lot quicker and easier. You need to wait another week before we do the procedure. I can get you in next Saturday morning. Will that

53

work, or would you prefer an afternoon appointment?" Rachel indicated that the latter would be preferable.

"Payment for all services is due up front. You'll need to bring $500 cash, $600 if you want the anesthesia (trust me, that's a really good deal). Every week you delay will add $100 to the cost. You're a smart girl, you can do the math. After sixteen weeks we can't perform the procedure here, so you'd have to go elsewhere at a more expensive cost," Candy stated. "If you want the anesthesia, make sure you don't eat twelve hours beforehand and that someone drives you home. Sign here." Candy was pushing a large document with lots of fine print in front of her. Rachel signed where Candy told her and the paperwork was complete.

Rachel's head was reeling from all that had happened in the past ten minutes. She knew from the reasons that she wrote down on the paper that she had every reason to abort, yet she was still confused. She walked out of the office and accidentally turned back into the examination room where her urine specimen still sat on the table with the pregnancy test still sticking out of it accusingly, like a testament to her irresponsibility, to her failure. She caught a glance of a familiar looking wrapper, which had been laid haphazardly on the tray next to it. The wrapper read, 'Pharmska Pregnancy Test, the most accurate value pregnancy test you can buy.'

Turning back out to exit the room, Rachel felt completely deceived by life. Betrayed by the manufacturer of the birth control pills, by that bastard Tom who got her pregnant, by life for having to drive a piece of garbage car, by the man who had taken advantage of her trust as an adolescent, and by the abortion clinic for making her lose half a day waiting and spending too much money for a cheap-ass pregnancy test when she already knew the results. But most of all, she felt stupid for not taking that girl Cari up on her offer of a free test that would have saved her money.

Exiting the abortion clinic, Rachel turned around to close the door behind her and noticed an impressive figure standing just a few feet away blocking the visibility to the sidewalk that led to where her car was parked.

II. Now and Then

Chapter 13

TIME: "Now"

"Come here please," a voice commanded. Rachel looked up and saw a stunning man whose chiseled features had an exotic appeal. His voice, although authoritative, held compassion in a way that compelled Rachel to obey. He was powerfully built, yet at the same time, there was a gentle aura that made Rachel feel safe in his presence. As Rachel moved toward him, all her fears and worries seemed to evaporate, and she had no choice but to obey that wonderful voice. Never looking away from him, she was more than happy to comply.

Looking into his blue eyes, Rachel asked, "Do I know you?" knowing full well that she had never seen him before. She would not have forgotten such a meeting under any circumstances.

"I'm Gabe," he replied without taking his eyes off her. Wearing a light grey cotton pin-stripe suit with a vibrant yellow and red silk tie and a white collared shirt, Gabe was not from this neighborhood. Though it was eighty-five degrees and humid, Gabe wasn't uncomfortable, and his smile radiated a sense of warmth. Rachel knew she was attracted to him but not in a physical way – more like how one is attracted to the beauty of a piece of art. "I've got a message for you," he continued.

A message for me? she thought, *it can't be from Tom since he could have just texted me, could it be from my mom,* she wondered.

"Jesus Christ loves you and Rita, and He will care for you both if you just trust in His goodness," Gabe said.

Oh great, another religious wacko. Rachel thought. "I'm sorry I don't have time for this," she said, turning away from him.

"Rachel," he said in a gentle but firm voice. Compelled, she turned and faced him again. "Jesus' mother Mary was in a crisis pregnancy situation, and she is praying for you to trust God the way she did. Go with Cari and her weirdo chorale. You can trust that they will help you." It was a simple message, but coming on the heels of the Jesus proclamation, Rachel wanted no part of it. She started to say, "Now listen here ..." but as she turned back toward Gabe, he was gone. "What the ...?" Rachel stammered as the most wonderful aroma of roses caught her attention. *Wow, I must be going nuts*, she thought, shaking her head. She shuttered at the implications. This was strange and scary, but that wonderful scent was intoxicating! Rachel wanted to stay in that spot some more and just drink in the scent of roses. Whatever else Gabe was, the guy was clearly a metro-sexual. Looking across the street at the strip mall, she noticed a green-and-red neon sign in Spanish and English that said:

Curandero Psychic friend $5 answers

That's what I need, someone to explain to me what's going on, Rachel thought. After a moment's reflection, a cold shiver went up Rachel's spine as she realized that she had not voiced the baby name 'Rita' to anyone, and yet Gabe said it. Nor had she ever verbalized the name she had come up with for Cari's singers. Realizing she had no money for a psychic reading, Rachel headed for her car.

"Hey gorgeous," Cari said, "are you ready to talk to us now?"

"Cari, what happened to your friend Gabe, the cute one?" Rachel asked.

"I'm not sure who you mean ... there are just us four out here right now," Cari replied gesturing to herself, the linebacker, the fat man, and the other two girls – five people. So Cari couldn't count either, Rachel thought.

"Stop messing with my head. You know the really great looking guy who talked to me over there. He told me to go with you." Rachel said as she pointed to the entrance of the abortion clinic.

"We never actually go on the property; we do all our work from the sidewalk. It must have been one of the homeless people. They all like us, and most of them know what we're about even if they don't always know which day it is or remember their own

57

names," Cari said smiling. "But he was right. You should come with us. I didn't catch your name earlier ..."

Before Rachel could reply, a shrill woman's voice called out, "Rachel, stay away from those liars!" It was Lucy. She had a look on her face that terrified Rachel. "These people just want to keep you down and prevent you from reaching your potential! Do you want to drive that piece of garbage car forever?" Lucy yelled in a derisive tone.

"I feel like we could use some help about now," the fat man said. Then the group on the sidewalk began reciting a prayer from memory,

> St. Michael the Archangel, defend us in battle,
> be our protection against the wickedness and
> snares of the devil. May God rebuke him, we
> humbly pray, and do thou, O prince of the
> heavenly hosts, by the power of God cast into
> hell Satan, and all the evil spirits who prowl
> through the world seeking the ruin of souls.

Lucy, visibly disturbed, must have been right behind Rachel now. Rachel could smell her. As Lucy reached out for Rachel, the big linebacker looking guy yelled, "NO TOUCHING!" He was quick. In no time he had gotten out of the line of people praying and was standing right up at the fence next to Cari. He stared straight at Lucy with a look on his face that said that not only wasn't he kidding, but that the fence he was leaning against was for him only a suggestion that he was not obligated to respect. Lucy cringed and cowered at this towering giant.

"Fine, Mike!" she shrieked. Clearly these two had history. "Just stay off my property," Lucy growled while trying to regain her composure. She obviously knew the linebacker and was afraid of him. She looked terribly flustered as she walked away and back towards the abortion clinic.

"C'mon, sweetie, what's your name?" Cari said, seemingly oblivious to the drama that had just transpired. *Apparently she was blind and deaf too*, Rachel thought.

"I'm Rachel," she replied, walking around the fence to join Cari and her band of misfits.

"Rachel, our shift is about finished here. This is Chris," she said, indicating the fat man. "He's going to pull up his truck for us and we're going to take you to a better place than this and get you some real help. Are you okay with that?"

"I don't know, I'm just confused right now," Rachel replied.

"Okay, are you hungry?"

"No, but I'm really thirsty," Rachel admitted. Cari reached into a little cooler and pulled out the last bottle of cold water for her. It was refreshing, and Rachel drank about 2/3 of it before stopping. "Oh, yes, that's what I needed," Rachel said. "I guess I'll go with you and see what you're talking about."

Chapter 14

TIME: "Eternity"

Let's look again at a closely related thread of time. Gabe communicated to Tammy as she reviewed one incident where she went to confession in the early 1990's:

Tammy, with her head covered by a white scarf, was waiting outside the confessional at Blessed Sacrament Catholic Church. One of the confessional doors opened and a person exited. A red light over the confessional turned green, meaning Tammy could now enter the confessional. She closed the door behind her, knelt facing the screen, and crossed herself as the small sliding door separating her from priest opened up. In a heavy Italian accent, the priest said "In the name of the Father, the Son and the Holy Spirit. May the Lord bless you and help you to make a good confession."

"Amen," Tammy replied. "Bless me, Father, for I have sinned. It has been five months since my last confession, and these are my sins: I have been impatient with my children, spent money unwisely, and lied to my husband about it. I have avoided my wifely duties, gossiped about my friends, and missed Mass too many times, Father."

"It seems like you may be holding something back?" said the voice on the other side of the screen. "How about forgiveness, do you have anger towards anybody? A religious figure perhaps, someone who made you do something you didn't want to do?" he asked, but Tammy had put it out of her mind.

"Not that I can remember, Father," she said, consciously making an effort to forget.

"Well, okay then. Please make an act of contrition but I can not give you absolution until you make a full, honest confession," the priest said. Tammy, shocked by the padre's revelation, left the church in tears, and never set foot in that parish again.

On her way home, she stopped by the hardware store to pick up some trash bags. A helpful sales girl named 'Candy' also talked her into buying a new garbage pail that she put in the truck and tied down with rope. As she was backing up, she misjudged the distance, backed into a new looking green F-150 pick up truck, and messed up the passenger side door. Tammy got out, cursing God and the older man driving the pickup truck with the now messed-up looking racing stripes. The young girl sitting on the passenger side of the truck looked mortified by the scene Tammy was making.

Another presence was with her and Gabe. It was Saint Pio. It had been him that she had gone to confession back then, but was completely unaware. She remembered thinking at the time that it was odd that a priest would suggest a sin to her when he did not know her, and then to have him not believe her lie and call her out for it – now she understood why. This was Jesus' way of reaching out to her in love and trying to get her to lay down the burden of anger she still carried.

By a special act of grace, Jesus had sent her Saint Pio, a confessor who had been bi-locating from another time and place. And not only had she held back, she had lied in the confessional. Then in that same hour, she had cursed God and her fellow man. Tammy was truly sorry and remorseful, and God knew it and she knew it. And in that same instant she felt everything around her change.

Instead of feeling just comfortable and peaceful, she was overwhelmed with joy and love, and knew that that feeling would never leave her. She was no longer alone with Gabe and Pio, she was together with all those who had gone before her – all her ancestors and friends who had died in a state of grace. They were all there, she could feel them and most importantly of all, HE was there with her. It was as if she felt His presence in that instant and knew He was saying, "Well done, My good and faithful servant. Because you have been responsible in little things, I have much greater things in store for you. You may now intercede for those you love, especially your children. Come, pray on their behalf, My precious one. Great is your reward."

61

Chapter 15

TIME: "Now"

Chris' truck was a rapidly aging green F-150 extended cab pickup with racing stripes that looked like it had had a rough life. It was roomy enough for the three of them and, most importantly, the air conditioner worked. Rachel was riding shotgun in the passenger seat while Cari continued talking from the backseat. Rachel half listened to her and half listened to the soft Christian music that played in the background.

"Weirdo chorale? That's friggin' hilarious, isn't it, Lardas?" Cari chuckled. Chris nodded his head ever so slightly and just kept smiling. "No Rachel, you just happened to come by in between sets of prayers. Our group follows a formal liturgy."

Cari caught Rachel's quizzical expression in the passenger side rear-view mirror and explained, "A liturgy is an ordered form of prayer service. The one that we follow was especially developed to be prayed in front of abortion clinics. A Catholic priest in New York named Monsignor Reilly along with his group called the Helpers of God's Precious Infants, started the prayer service. In between each set of prayers, we sing a song with a pro-life theme. You just happened to come along when we were singing 'Silent Night', which, yeah, I guess I can see how that could make us seem a little weird. Next time you should join in and help us sound better," she laughed.

Rachel liked Cari. She was very positive, upbeat, and she seemed like a really fun person – a little too wholesome maybe, but very engaging and entertaining. Cari had a knack for pushing the envelope, of broaching subjects that were uncomfortable or socially awkward, but she did it in such a light-hearted, non-abrasive way that it was really disarming.

"I think you should name the baby Rita," Cari declared.

"Now wait a minute! What's going on here? Are you guys some kind of psychics or something?"

"What do you mean?" Cari asked innocently.

62

"When I was a little girl playing dolls with my sisters, my favorite doll I had was named Rita. I've always liked the name, and thought that one day, if I had a daughter, I'd call her Rita. Nobody I hang around with these days would even know that, but in the last ten minutes both you and your buddy Gabe knew the name I would have given to a daughter. Something isn't right here. So, do you read minds, or what?" Rachel said with conviction.

"I'm sorry, Rachel. It's like I told you, I don't know any street person named Gabe, or anyone else for that matter. Put your mind at rest, please, because no, I cannot read it," Cari laughed at the play on words and so did Rachel, picking up on it right away. Apparently they had the same sense of humor. "That's the first name that came to my mind – Rita. So, if you've heard it from someone else recently, then maybe it is confirmation that this is what is supposed to be."

"Here we go, ladies," said Chris, pulling the old truck up to a parking spot in front of a dilapidated old building. *What a dump*, Rachel thought. Two front windows were boarded up along with another one on the side of the building. A front window was also partially covered in plastic. Graffiti artists supplied the paint job with their creativity. Out front, a couple of guys were carrying a sofa through the front door – although from the looks of the sofa, they should have been heading out, not in.

"You're joking, right?" asked Rachel. "This doesn't look like a crisis pregnancy center to me," she said, fumbling in her purse for her can of mace. Rachel's mind started to go into overdrive. *Did they put something in the water bottle? Are they planning on doing something to me once we're inside?* She couldn't think straight.

Chris started laughing. "Please excuse our appearance, we're re-modeling."

"Don't joke, Chris! Can't you see she's nervous?" Cari said. "Rachel, we are a low budget operation subsidized entirely by the Church and private donations. Our clinic is actually in the back. The front part is being used to house donated items for the St Vincent DePaul Society for the store over on Sassafras

63

Street. This was the only space we could afford, and we were lucky to get it, since the diocese just cut back our budget. Unlike the place you just came from, Rachel, we're all volunteers and do what we can. If you think about it, there really is a huge inequity in how both places operate. When someone chooses abortion, AAA gets money. When someone chooses life, we actually lose money because we give away free resources to help the mother and child in crisis."

Rachel started to see the difference between the abortion clinic and this organization. This was run on the generosity of donations, while the clinic made money from abortions. Rachel was beginning to see what type of conviction it took from these people to help others, and began to respect it. Chris got out, opened the passenger side doors for Rachel and Cari, and said, "I have to run a few errands, so call me when you're ready to go back."

"Thanks, Chris, see you later," Cari said. The girls walked around the side and Rachel noticed a tasteful, handmade sign attached to the building with a picture of a mother and child and an arrow pointing towards the back of the building. The girls went into the back door and walked past a sign saying, 'Catholic Charities Pregnancy Center.' She welcomed the comfortable and familiar rush of air conditioning that hit her whole body in a refreshing burst.

"Emma!" Cari called.

"Hi Cari, you brought someone to visit with us today?" a friendly smiling voice said from the back room. Emma walked out and greeted Cari with a friendly hug.

"Emma, this is my new friend Rachel," Cari said, introducing her. The phrase 'new friend' was a pre-arranged code word that this was someone in a crisis pregnancy situation who she had most likely just brought in from the abortion clinic.

"Great to meet you, Rachel!" Emma said enthusiastically, while gently but firmly shaking her hand. "Come on over and have a seat so we can talk!" She guided Rachel over to a sitting area

64

with a couple of worn but clean, functional sofas. Clearly this was a low budget operation, maybe even a no-budget operation, but at least it was clean, didn't smell bad, and the people were nice. The contrast between this environment and the abortion clinic was night and day. A phrase came to her mind as she pondered this mental juxtaposition: *you clean the outside of the cup and dish, but inside you are full of greed and wickedness. This must be some metaphor from an old movie she had seen once, she supposed, or was it from a play.* No matter, it sure fit here.

"So Rachel, do you know for sure if you are pregnant?" Emma asked. "We could test you now," she offered, handing Rachel a tray with four hermetically sealed pregnancy tests. Rachel recognized the writing on the wrapper instantly: *Pharmska Pregnancy Test, the most accurate value pregnancy test you can buy.*

"No thanks, I've failed four of them already."

"You mean you passed them," Emma corrected. "When a woman is with child that means that she succeeded and her body systems are working the way they were designed."

That phrase 'with child' caught Rachel off guard. So did the way Emma had phrased everything. For the first time, here was someone who thought about things in a way that was totally foreign to the culture that Rachel had been raised in. The implications were profound yet deliriously simple: sex was for making babies. She had made a baby; therefore, she succeeded in doing what her body was meant to do. *Wow.*

"Let's take a look at your baby, shall we?" Emma said, still smiling as she got up and offered Rachel her hand. Rachel accepted the hand and followed Emma to a room in the back. The room looked pretty much like any other medical facility she had ever been in – clean, blank walls. There was a crucifix by the door and a poster of beautiful babies of every ethnicity wearing different colored sleepers and a quote from the late Mother Teresa which read, "How can there be too many babies, that is like saying there are too many flowers?" The décor was spartan but functional; a couple of folk-art paintings on the wall,

65

but most importantly it was clean. There was an examination table with a clean sheet of tissue paper pulled over it, and an ultrasound device hooked up to a laptop.

"Here is a gown. I'll leave you alone while you put it on. Here are a couple of bottles of water. We'll need for you to drink these first, since the ultrasound works best in an early pregnancy if you've got a full bladder. So go ahead and drink both of those first. Then wait a couple of minutes and call out to me when you're ready," Emma said. Rachel didn't hear much other activity going on in the place, just Cari talking to someone else in the reception area. It sounds like she was the only patient today so there was no long wait at all. Rachel did as instructed and, getting up on the examination table, called when she was ready.

Emma came back into the room with another lady, a short-haired brunette in blue scrubs and a white lab coat.

"Hi Rachel, I'm Diane, the ultrasound technician," she said smiling. "Go ahead and lie down while I calibrate the machine, it'll only take a minute." Diane began tapping away on the laptop and adjusting the cables, while a device on the wall began to hum softly. After a couple of minutes, she pushed the power button on a large 17" monitor that was suspended by a mechanical metal arm, and moved it away from the wall so that all three of them could see it.

Putting on a clean pair of gloves, Diane continued. "Go ahead and move your gown," and Rachel complied. "I'm going to put some of this gel on your belly. It's going to feel a little cold at first."

Eeek, Rachel thought as the gel went on, *that WAS cold. Thanks for the warning*, she said silently as she smiled at Diane.

"Now let's see who we've got here," Diane said as she placed the plastic and metal ultrasound transducer onto the gelled area over Rachel's womb. The visual on the screen was unclear at first, black and white with some little number on the side of the screen that Rachel didn't understand. But then it came into focus as Diane turned dials and typed on the laptop, and the color came on.

"It looks like you're between six and seven weeks," Diane observed. "See, there's the head," she said, pointing it out to Rachel. "And you can't really see the heart beating with an untrained eye at this stage, but the equipment can, and our transducer is reporting that your baby's heartbeat is between 90-110 beats per minute – which is what is typically seen at this stage."

Rachel was floored. On the screen right in front of her, was the child in her womb. "They told me at AAA that it was just a mass of cells but this is a real baby. They lied to me. Why would they do that?"

"Rachel, if you were to use their abortion services, how much money would you have had to pay them?" Emma asked. Then it hit Rachel why they lied. *Of course. It was a cash business, and that was all they cared about. Why should they tell her the truth? That's why they didn't offer to let her see an ultrasound.*

"Can you tell what the sex is?" Rachel asked hopefully.

"Not at this point, but we'll have you come back in a few weeks and we'll do all of that with you," Diane said.

"Diane is recording all of this and making a CD for you to show everybody your baby. You can overlay an MP3 on it and make a music video out of it if you like."

67

Chapter 16

TIME: "Now"

"Rachel, is that you?" her mother Ruth's voice called out from the kitchen. "Are you here for dinner?" It was a fair question, given that Rachel pretty much didn't take most meals with the family anymore.

"Yeah, Mom, what're we having?" Rachel replied.

"Poor man's feast!" which was one of her Mom's best dishes and the easiest one to make, since all she had to do was put a pot roast, potatoes, carrots and spices into a Crock-pot before she left for work in the morning and take it out at dinner time. She called it a, 'Poor man's feast' because she was able to feed a family of six on it for less than ten dollars. Ruth had learned many ways of stretching the family's money over the years.

TIME: "Then"

Ruth had grown up in foster care, spending her early years drifting from one foster family to another, sometimes for good reason, sometimes for no discernable reason. She had gotten used to social workers – 'people movers' as she called them – shifting her from place to place, and had always longed for stability and family. She had finally succeeded in creating a family and added stability with her latest husband. Ruth didn't usually pick things up very quickly, usually by trial and error, and had accumulated much wisdom and street smarts over her thirty-five years.

As a young child, one of her foster mothers had warned her not to touch the hot stove, but Ruth had done it anyway. Some things are felt right away, such as the pain of a burned hand, while inner pain takes much longer to feel. Ruth had been both blessed and cursed with good looks. Her daughters' friends always told them that she looked like she could be Brittany Spears older sister. Ruth found out both boys and men were attracted to her, and a foster home wasn't necessarily a safe haven, especially when a foster father goes too far.

Ruth had never really been nurtured as a child and did not have a positive male father figure in her life who loved her just for who she was. Without a good family to help nurture her, she was an emotional cripple whose development was scarred by events that took place. She found that she had always been attracted to much older men – she saw in their affection and attention something that she had lacked her whole life. Without a sense of identity and security to help her learn to love herself, she wasn't able to develop and appreciate the unique gifts that she had. Instead, she learned to think of herself as a collection of body parts that men desired to use for their pleasure.

It had started with a foster brother when she was fourteen. His name was Danny. He was seventeen years old and just a few months away from legal emancipation. 'Bubba,' as he liked to be called, had paid lots of attention to her, and she liked it. He made her feel special, and listened to her when she spoke and never ridiculed her. He was strong and took care of her whenever other kids started to bother her. The physical touching started innocently enough, but over the ensuing weeks it became more daring and she liked it. Once intercourse started, Ruth felt like a grown up because Bubba made her feel special. It was inevitable that the other kids in the house began to take notice of how much time they were spending together and even snickered about it behind their backs. It wasn't long before word got back to the foster parents that something might be going on. One day, their foster father Elmer had come home from work early and caught the two of them in bed together. The people movers came over within the hour and Bubba had been moved to another place.

That night Elmer explained to Ruth that Bubba's removal was in her best interest, and promised to be more attentive to her. He kept that promise, but not in the way that he should have. At first it was subtle, running into her just as Ruth came out of the bathroom after showering or entering her room, which had no lock, without knocking just as she was getting dressed. Of course, he apologized for forgetting to knock, so Ruth didn't think much about it. His hugs started to get longer, more frequent, and more licentious. Elmer began taking her shopping for clothes, although he rarely bought her anything. Instead, he'd have her try on provocative clothes and come out of the dressing room to show him. Occasionally Elmer would buy her a revealing outfit that made Ruth happy. He would then take pictures of her from different angles and gradually the clothes came off. Then one night when her foster mother had taken all the other kids out to the high school homecoming, Ruth stayed home with a headache. Elmer decided to stay home with her, and once they were alone he made his move. Ruth, excited by the forbidden attention and affection, consented to his overtures.

This was not Elmer's first time having a tryst with a foster child entrusted to his care. Elmer was a predator, but since no girls had ever complained, as far as the community was concerned he was an upstanding citizen who was very giving of his time and did a great job of mentoring the less fortunate. For Elmer and his wife, fostering kids was a business – most of their household income derived from the state subsidies they received. They held part-time jobs to supplement the income, and stay connected to the community – but behind the façade was a child predator who knew which girls were most vulnerable to his advances. Elmer was calculating and patient, and knew how to manipulate the girls until he got what he wanted.

Elmer worked as a night auditor for a local motel, and there were times when Ruth would go there under some pretense of bringing him an item he forgot. This gave him the opportunity to use one of the rooms with Ruth. Elmer manipulated Ruth into keeping the affair quiet, telling her that he'd be killed if anyone found out and that it would be all her fault. Ruth felt confused by her feelings, guilt and sympathy mixed together in what she thought was love. There were some days when Elmer got home in the morning and his wife left for work. Ruth would stay with him for a couple hours, whereupon an excused note from her foster father was always sufficient to get her back into school tardy. Ruth was always careful when to say 'Dad' and when to say 'Elmer,' something that helped her become a good actress of sorts.

Her pregnancy caught her by surprise. She had never really thought about it – the idea of getting pregnant – but she welcomed it. Finally, there was going to be someone who no one else could take away from her! When she broke the news to Elmer, though, he did not act the way she thought he would. She had just finished bringing him his lunch at the hotel that he had 'forgotten,' and after she took care of his real hunger, she broke it to him, "Elmer, I'm pregnant."

"Are you sure?" he asked.

"Yes, I took one of those tests they sell at the drugstore, and it turned the blue color, which explains why I missed my period the last two times. I thought maybe it was just stress."

"Obviously, this is not supposed to happen. You'll need to get an abortion." Ruth was stunned at what she was hearing.

"But I want a baby of my own," she protested.

"But I don't," he said with a note of finality.

"I have a friend over in the city that can help us out. He and I like to swap pictures from the magazines like I showed you. You know, SPECIAL pictures like we took that time," he winked.

"Dr. Ike Cutter owes me one. I'll give him a call in the morning and see if I can get you an appointment for Saturday. It goes without saying, 'mum's the word'. Now get on home."

Ruth was scared – no, she was terrified. She felt rejected, used, and discarded, and she knew that he was serious about making her have an abortion. She would never agree to that, so she knew she had to leave. When she got back to the house, everyone else was still asleep in bed, so she tiptoed over to the phone book in the kitchen and picked up the yellow pages. Sitting herself down, she looked under 'abortion' and found three full page ads for abortion clinics before finding what she thought she needed under abortion alternatives: 'Catholic Charities Pregnancy Center.' She didn't have a pen, so she just carefully

71

and quietly tore the page out that had the phone number, and put it in her pocket before tiptoeing back to bed. There was a phone booth between the house and her school, so she would place a call in the morning.

"Hi, I need help," Ruth said in a child-like voice.

"Good! That's why we're here. My name is Emma, how can I help you today?" a cheery woman's voice replied.

"I'm pregnant by my foster father, and he said he was going to take me to Dr. Cutter to make me have an abortion this Saturday, and I want to keep my baby," Ruth said as the words rushed out of her mouth.

"First of all, you need to know Ruth that submitting to abortion is a woman's choice and no one, not your parents, not your boyfriend, his parents, a teacher, nor a preacher, not even your husband, can legally make you do it. Can you get over to our crisis pregnancy center?" Emma asked.

"No, I live out in the county, just down from the Sheepaz Motel on Highway 60. I don't drive," Ruth replied.

"Okay, I don't have anyone who can get out there right now, so here's what we're going to do. I have an idea ... Operation Rescue is going to be holding a rally at Dr. Cutter's clinic this Saturday." Emma said as she detailed a plan of action.

Saturday morning came, and Elmer had told his wife that he was taking Ruth into town to run some errands. Ruth had been instructed by Elmer to bring a change of loose – fitting clothing, which Dr. Cutter's office had suggested she would need for after the procedure, so she had a small overnight bag under her shoulder as they got in his truck and took off. Elmer loved this new truck. It was a few years old but it was new to him. His 'new' truck was a green Ford F-150 extended cab with racing stripes all the way down the sides – it was cool. He paid for the truck through his family business of taking in foster kids, and, of course, victimizing them with impunity. Elmer loved this job!

72

"This really is for the best, Ruth. You'll feel so much better afterwards," he said, putting his hand on her knee. The distraction caused Elmer to go through a red light and tear off the rear bumper of a cherry-red mustang that had been cruising through on the crossroad. CRASH!!! The sickening sound of metal being wrenched from metal was heard for a whole block. Elmer and Ruth, wearing seatbelts, were stunned but unhurt. Getting out to inspect the damage, Elmer was glad to see that his truck got away pretty unscathed. "Are you alright?" he asked going over to the other car where an attractive, professional-looking black woman in her early twenties was sitting.

"I think so," she replied. "You missed that light didn't you?"

"Yes, Miss, I did, let me get my insurance information for you. Here is my driver's license," he said, handing her his license. Her rear chrome bumper had been completely ripped off. It was a nice car – a classic 67 that had been completely restored. *Parts for those vehicles were getting hard to come by; this would not be cheap to repair,* he thought taking note of the odd vanity plate on the dislocated bumper that said, "NOT REDY."

After dealing with the accident, Elmer kept his hands on the wheel.

"I have one more stop before we get to the clinic. I need some three-fourths inch brads at the hardware store. It shouldn't take but a minute," he said, whizzing by an old cathedral into the parking lot of a small, family-run hardware store. CRASH!

Some crazy woman with a stupid trashcan hanging off the back of her car wasn't looking and backed into him. Now Elmer was really off kilter. He got out and started yelling at the woman, who was giving it right back to him. Ruth just cringed, and started crying as Elmer hollered at the poor woman who had run into him. She had put a dent in the side of the truck and really scratched up the racing stripe on that side. It was just cosmetic, but it didn't look good, and having two accidents in one day was not going to impress Elmer's insurance company.

After the second accident, Elmer was really on edge, so Ruth kept quiet for the remainder of the trip. Dr. Cutter's place was a cute little office that looked like it used to be a house in a run down part of town, and there was some kind of drama going on. There were police and protesters and picket signs – all things that made Elmer very nervous. He parked the truck in one of the spaces and was helped out by a beautiful blond lady.

"Hi Elmer, I'm Lucy," she said. "Dr. Cutter is expecting you so just stay on the walkway and ignore all those troublemakers over there, and everything will be fine," she said, smiling.

Elmer was now doubly nervous. He was not used to beautiful, adult women paying attention to him, and this one was HOT! Elmer liked to be in control, and this, on top of the two accidents he had just been in, really disturbed his internal equilibrium. Just then, he caught a whiff of the vilest scent. UGH! It was coming from this woman, and it was overpowering!

"Ok, thank you," he said, closing the door and heading toward the sidewalk.

Wow! What was going on here? It looked like a modeling contest or something; there were gorgeous hot women in skimpy outfits all over this place, but their eyes were all weird – hollow, empty, and dark, just frickin' weird, but hell, he thought, *who needs eyes when they're built like that!* Elmer looked over to the sidewalk where the protesters were and saw that some of the hot chicks were wrapped around some of the police, and even one or two of the protesters … it looked like they were all whispering in their ears – how kinky! Most of the people out there had contorted faces, as if they had just smelled something awful or thought of something very disturbing. Elmer figured the police must have used a stink bomb or something on the protesters. Just then, Lucy came up, grabbed him around the waist, and whispered in his ear.

"Get on with it! Do what you came here for." Elmer's ear tickled and a sick smile came to his face.

"C'mon, Ruth, let's get a move on, Get out of the car!" he barked.

Ruth was a bundle of nerves, her feelings about Elmer were all confused, but she knew one thing for sure: there was no way she was going to submit to an abortion. She remembered the instructions that Emma had given her. She opened the door and made as if she was walking toward the clinic just a step behind Elmer and Lucy. Then she abruptly made a turn toward the line of policemen standing between the protesters and the clinic ... Lucy saw her break and ran after her.

"Harry! Jana! Lupe! Abe! I feel like we need some extra protection out here," a young man named Chris with a moustache and dark glasses called out from the sidewalk, at which most of the pro-life people on the sidewalk responded, "Saint Michael the Archangel, defend us in battle, be our protection against the wickedness and snares of the devil ...."

Lucy came screaming like a bat out of hell. "Get back here, you little ..." SMASH! Lucy's momentum was stopped by the chest of a huge linebacker-type, the biggest guy Elmer had ever seen, as he physically blocked her from touching Ruth. The police didn't seem to care at all. Did they see what was going on?

"May God rebuke him we humbly pray ..." the pro-life people continued.

At once the linebacker drew back his massive fist and sucker punched a befuddled Lucy, who fell to the ground at Elmer's feet. He quickly stepped back and watched the wild scene unfold.

The chorus of voices continued, "And do thou, O prince of the heavenly host, by the power of God, cast into hell Satan, and all the evil spirits ..." Suddenly, a group of aggressive football player types each well over six-feet tall and powerfully built, came seemingly out of nowhere and started grabbing the strange-looking models whose whispers turned to shrieks of fear and pure terror as they were torn away from the people they had been clinging to and cast off to the side. Most of them fled instantly while others slowly got up and moved as a group back into the clinic, including Lucy. Still the police did nothing as they stood motionless on the street – seemingly oblivious to it all.

"...who prowl through the world, seeking the ruin of souls. Amen," the people finished.

"Ruth, what are you doing! Get over here, girl!" Elmer said, coming after her.

He caught her arm just as she said, "Officer, I am a ward of the state living in foster care. I am a victim of statutory rape at the hands of this man who is my foster father."

"You little liar!" Elmer screamed, slapping her across the face so forcefully that she fell to the ground. Before he could come down for a second strike, his arms were pinned behind him by one of the police. "You have the right to remain silent. Anything you say can and will be used against you in a court of law."

"You little @#$%$^@^&%^#" Elmer cussed up a storm. One of the police officers standing nearby took out a hand held tape recorder and said, "So what do you think of the judge's mother?" before putting the microphone in Elmer's livid face. "@#% #$# !!^%$%@# " Elmer opined as the cop shook his head and laughed. "Got it, Sarge!"

"Sergeant, my name is Emma, and this is my friend Stacy, who's a licensed social worker. We're here to help that young girl who is a victim of sexual assault. Her name is Ruth. Would you please let her come to us?" Emma inquired sweetly to the officer in charge of the operations out there, handing him her card while Stacy flashed her credentials.

"Certainly, ma'am, but we'll need for her to come down to the station in a while to give a statement. You can be with her when she does, if she agrees."

"Thank you, officer, that will be just fine. Ruth, it's Emma. Come here, dear," she said while waving her hand.

"I didn't want to hurt him," Ruth cried.

"It's okay, dear, you didn't hurt him. He hurt you. You're the victim here, not him – you and your poor little baby. Let me look at your face, it's a little swollen. Let's go get you some ice," Emma said as she led her toward the police car.

Ruth was not a very religious person considering her background in the foster care system. One of the foster families she had as a young child was Catholic and had her baptized, so on any form which asked for religious preference, she always put 'Catholic.' But other than a few times as a youngster, she had never really been to church and never thought of going. She knew that Emma and her people would gladly take her if she wanted to go, but they were careful not to push it. They were not shy about sharing the blessings they had received from going to church; however they did not tie any strings to the assistance they offered her.

Over the ensuing days, Emma and her volunteer helpers made several appointments for Ruth to see doctors for pre-natal care and various social service agencies, and they shuffled her around a couple of temporary housing situations while they waited for a space to open up at a special home for unwed mothers. Since Ruth was a ward of the state, getting her in was relatively easy from a paperwork standpoint, since she was already 'in the system.'

Elmer went to jail. He was charged with assault on a minor, child endangerment, child rape, resisting arrest, and several other things. He was facing 25 years if convicted. Fortunately, for him, he got a very sympathetic judge who liked the fact that he had dedicated so much of his life to helping underprivileged kids and let him plead out to child endangerment and lascivious conduct. He got six months suspended sentence and was then told he had to perform 400 hours of community service. He did his service time volunteering as a birth control counselor for Planned Patrimony at a local girl's camp.

Six months after Ruth's daughter Rachel was born, she took her infant daughter out for a walk one day in a baby carriage

77

borrowed from the home for young mothers in crisis and never returned. At fifteen, Ruth's marketable skills were very limited, so she found herself doing like most other uneducated people, trading her labor in blocks of time for money. An attractive girl, she quickly found a man who gave her a place to live in exchange for having his needs met. She lied about her age and got a job working in the kitchen of an Indian restaurant. At first she just washed the dishes, but after a while she began helping with food preparation, and even learned a few things about slow cooking that she retained and used over the years.

Eventually, she left the guy, and moved in with another young mother. They split living expenses while watching each others babies and worked opposite shifts. It worked out fine for a couple of years, until the other girl got a boyfriend who started interfering with the schedule that they had worked out, and ultimately convinced her roommate to move in with him instead.

By then, Ruth had turned eighteen and gotten a job as a cocktail waitress, which had briefly introduced her to the world of alcohol and well-dressed, successful men. Since she was very attractive, this could have opened up some other possibilities for her. But one night, after drinking too many 'samples,' she had gone home with the cute new bartender and Rachel's sister Maggie was conceived. What Ruth had intended to be a one-night stand dragged out into a stress-filled, yearlong relationship with a man whose personality was far less disarming when he wasn't drinking or hustling tips behind a bar.

Ruth lost her job once she began to show. In the world of nightclubs, where alcohol and pretty girls were the main attraction, being pregnant did not mix well in the eyes of management. She was dismissed on a trumped up charge of being late, although everyone knew it was just a thinly veiled excuse. Cocktail lounges were for people to relax and fantasize, and attractive, friendly waitresses were there as a distraction from real life. Pregnancy was real life, and did nothing for the illusion or ambiance. With no other source of income, Ruth went on public assistance, which paid for Maggie's birth, so it worked out. Soon after little Maggie was born, her father announced that he needed his space, and once again Ruth was on her own, only this time with two little girls.

Ruth regained her figure fairly rapidly after Margaret was born; due more to a poor diet than any fitness training. Once Margaret was able to sleep through the night, Ruth knew she was in over her head, and thought that she needed a man to help her out of her current situation. Of course she knew by now that any good looking woman who wanted to find a man could do so with minimal effort, but she hadn't yet been burned enough to realize that the place she looked for a man might have something to do with the type of guy she attracted.

After securing some part time baby-sitting services for her daughters, Ruth got a job cocktail waitressing in a strip club. This particular club required that she dress in lingerie so men would slip 'tips' into her clothing, but it did not require her to completely disrobe. Ruth loved the attention she got at this place, and the way the men who came to this environment threw bills around often gave the illusion that they had more money than they really did. She found that she could relate to many of the girls who worked there. Some were hopelessly addicted to drugs and others came from situations much like hers. Every now and then one of the girls might come in with a fat lip or black eye, and all the other girls would gather round and help her cover the marks up with makeup and listen to the horror stories about what this boyfriend or that husband did.

Ruth was happy here, and she had occasion to accept several invitations to go out 'after hours' with men who tipped exceptionally well. One guy who she got together with had come in one night throwing $20 bills around like they were confetti. After a few drinks, Ruth went home with him to his dumpy little apartment. The next morning he informed her that he had just blown all that money from an insurance settlement he had received from an on-the-job accident. Not only didn't he have any more money, but he couldn't work either, and was on disability. Ruth felt sorry for him, and saw a benefit in the disability check he was able to bring in without working, so she moved him into her place and conceived Rachel's second sister, Fatima.

79

This relationship led to a civil marriage and some form of home stability for Ruth as she continued to work nights at the club. A disabled husband meant that she could now work full time – five nights per week since not only did she have his check to count on, but a free, built-in babysitter. As long as his glass was kept full, he was fine with the situation. Over the months and years, Ruth learned to refine the art of flirtatious seduction at the club. She would leave for work each night at six and her husband would usually start drinking about that time, so for the next couple of hours, her daughters' primary care giver would be sober enough until they went to bed. To them, this became the norm, and along with it, the mood swings and erratic behavior of an intoxicated care giver. On a rough night, Ruth might come home at two or three in the morning to find some glass or bottle dropped or smashed against the tile floor, and her husband passed out in a heap on the table or on the floor with the girls all huddled together. Sleeping in one bedroom with the door locked, Rachel clinging to that porcelain doll she called 'Rita' that Ruth had found for her at a yard sale.

As unfavorable as her circumstances might seem, Ruth was very optimistic by nature, in part because she did not always understand the options she had or the gravity of the challenges she faced most of the time. For her, ignorance truly was bliss of some sort. Due to the socio-economic circles she traveled in, she was always blessed by the presence of people who were worse off than she was (at least in her opinion), and that made her challenges seem more bearable. Her husband would often entertain his friends at their apartment in the evenings, and most of them were in similar circumstances – heavy drinkers, unstable emotionally and mentally, and virtually unemployable for one reason or another. One evening when he was playing cards with his brother, he passed out early and his brother took advantage of the situation to empty his wallet, take some fake jewelry that Ruth had in their bedroom (he thought it was real), and molest Rachel. When Ruth found out about what happened from her scared and crying thirteen-year-old daughter, Ruth went ballistic and kicked her husband out on the street. Two restraining orders and fourteen months later she was completely free of him.

One evening, when Ruth was catching a quick bite to eat at Freddy's Fish Fry next to where she worked, she was surprised by the forwardness of a strange but very intriguing older gentleman in a clean suit who came up to her table.

"You should try the garlic fish liver melt. It doesn't have the best flavor, but it does keep the vampires away. I'm Ralph. May I join you?" Ralph was polite, respectful, and looking at her eyes when he spoke. Ruth was not used to that and she liked it.

"Sure, be my guest," she smiled. She had not yet changed into her 'cocktail uniform,' which was in the shopping bag beside her that also contained her purse.

"Grabbing a quick bite before work? You have the look of someone whose day is just beginning," he said, smiling.

"Yes, I'm on my way to the office next door. Are you heading over there too?" Ruth asked.

"No disrespect intended madam but no, that establishment is not on my itinerary – not this evening nor any other time. I'm actually on my way to meet an old friend who I haven't seen in a while, and this is the only place I know that makes fish gizzard treats," he said, popping a salty French fry into his mouth and quickly swallowing before continuing. "This friend of mine is in kind of a bind. You see, his woman left him with a four-year-old daughter, and he works odd hours as a private investigator, so he never knows when he will be coming and going and hasn't been able to find a steady babysitter. So, he's really reaching out to everyone to help him at this time, and it appears that his repertoire of friends is running a bit thin these days, because I've been asked to look after his daughter tonight. It's a bit out of the ordinary for me, as you might imagine," he chuckled amicably.

Ralph's honest and friendly demeanor really struck her as special for some reason that she couldn't quite explain. He seemed to be a very decent man, better than the ones she dealt with each night, and the kind of friend anyone would be lucky to have. If his friend were anything like him then he might be worth

81

knowing too. Ralph bowed his head briefly and silently clasped his hands for a moment. *He must be saying grace,* she thought – *how sweet.* Just then, someone she recognized from her past came through the door and caught her eye. The recognition was mutual and instantaneous.

"Emma!" she called out, getting up so quickly that she spilled her fries on the ground and knocked her drink over sideways. Thank heavens for plastic lids; the loss of diet cola was minor and easily contained.

"Oh my goodness! Ruth right?! How long has it been – must be 14 or 15 years? My, you're so grown up and you're so pretty! You came to us at that final Rescue rally back before the F.A.C.E act passed," Emma said, lovingly taking her in her arms like a mother hen wrapping up her chick in the warmth of her wings. She felt wonderful to Ruth. Right down to that same sweet perfume she still wore. "I'd recognize that beautiful face anywhere, Ruth. It's so good to see you. I didn't know you knew Ralph."

"Well, we've just met."

"Ralph, how are you, dear? Are you out on a big mission tonight?" Emma said, winking at him and exchanging friendly kisses.

"If you see me out at night then you know I'm doing a big one. By the way, my boss sends you his love, but I know you don't need me to tell you that Emma, since you talk to him as often as I do – maybe more?" he said as they both laughed at some inside joke that went over Ruth's head.

"Is there anything I can do to help you, Ralph? You know I'd do anything to help you," Emma said earnestly.

"You've already done it, dear. You're the best!" Ralph replied.

"Well, I can see that you're busy, Ralph, so I'll just do what I came here to do. I took your advice about nuking the fish gizzards when I got home from here the last time and you were right – it made the biggest difference! I felt wonderful after that! I'm feeling like doing it again tonight when I get back home," Emma said. "Ruth, here is my card. Please call me. We absolutely need to get together again. My office has been moved, but you can reach me on my new cell phone anytime. I finally got one of these things, I feel like I can't work it half the time, but my husband set it up for me to just press one button to call the numbers I call all the time. So it works for at least nine people," Emma laughingly said, handing Ruth her card. Emma waved good-bye to both of them as she went over to the window marked 'pick up orders only' and was waited on by a young looking teenage boy whose big bright name tag said 'Stevie.' Behind her in line was a naughty little girl who couldn't have been more than eight or nine in a catholic school uniform whose mother was having a hard time getting her to behave.

"Mommy, I want a princess fish head doll! A green one Mommy, not a pink one!" the little girl screamed.

"Shhh, be quiet, Catherine or I swear you won't get anything!" her flustered mother said in a very controlled tone of voice that belied how stressed she felt by the commotion her daughter was making.

Ruth held Emma in very high regard for all the help she had given her so long ago. If Ralph was a friend of Emma's, then her instincts about him must be true. He had to be trustworthy. As they sat back down to finish Ruth asked, "So your friend is a P.I. What do you do, Ralph?"

"I manage a courier service, so I seldom have to make deliveries myself. I do have others working under me, but every now and then when the client is big enough, I'll take on the job myself. And as it happens, I have one such client tonight, so I won't be able to help my friend out the way he thinks." Ralph said sadly putting a round and gritty fried fish gizzard covered in Cajun spicy cocktail sauce into his mouth.

83

"Well, as luck would have it, I can go into work a little late today, it's Wednesday, and our regulars go to church first, so it'll be slow for a couple of hours. If you pay for a phone call, I think I can help you and your friend tonight. I have a fifteen-year-old who can babysit his little girl while she looks after her little sisters. Can you personally vouch for your friend?" Ruth asked.

"Absolutely, this gentleman has a heart of gold. You're gonna love him," Ralph promised. "Here's my cell phone. As soon as you're done, we can take my car."

After they finished eating, Ralph and Ruth walked out to his vehicle. Ruth couldn't place the make and model, but it was white and classy looking, and appeared to have been spit-polished. Even in the parking lot with poor lighting, she could tell this car belonged to someone very wealthy and very important. Ralph opened the passenger-side door for her and walked around to get in on the driver's side. The interior had every option you could want, and it just felt so warm and safe and luxurious inside.

"Wow, this is some set of wheels!" Ruth remarked.

"It's a custom job, one of a kind. It belongs to my boss," Ralph said. "I only use it for special jobs, like the one I'm working tonight. I think of it as a little piece of heaven," he said, winking. They drove for about fifteen minutes out into the suburbs. Ruth had been living in the city for so long with no car that she rarely went anywhere off the bus lines. She had forgotten how nice it was outside the city. They pulled up in front of a small bungalow that had its front porch light on – clearly a house that was expecting company. Ever the gentleman, Ralph got out and opened the door for Ruth and led the way up the little porch stairs to knock on the front door. A decent but unremarkable looking man answered it with a smile.

"Oh Ralph, I'm so glad to see you. Who is this lovely lady?" he said, focusing on Ruth. Ruth liked him right away. He was a few inches taller than her, had a great smile, was dressed decently, and seemed very genuine and friendly.

"Toby, I'd like to introduce you to my new friend, Ruth. I'm sorry to tell you this, Toby, but I've been called into work on crucial business, so I can't baby-sit for you tonight. But Ruth has a teenage daughter who is available so I brought her over for you two to discuss it."

"Please come in," Toby said.

Toby was apprehensive about having Ruth's daughter baby-sit when he found out where Ruth worked, but he was desperate, and it would just be for about three hours, so he didn't really feel like he had much of a choice. He had to follow up on something for a client, and the only chance there would be to do it was tonight. Toby took comfort in the fact that Ralph was suggesting it. Ralph was someone he didn't see very often, but he was also someone Toby had known ever since he could remember. Ralph had been friends with his parents, and it had been Ralph who told him about his grandfather's death when he was a kid. His parents had asked for his help in breaking the sad news to Toby. Come to think of it, how old was Ralph anyway? He couldn't say that he was really close with Ralph, but he could definitely say that his trust in him was absolute. Come to think of it, family funerals were about the most common time he remembered seeing Ralph. If Ralph suggested something, then it would be okay.

"If we're all in agreement, then I have to get going. Toby, Ruth can give you directions back to her place so Rachel can watch Suzy. Goodnight, everyone," he said, feigning to tip an imaginary hat. As the group drove over to Ruth's place, Toby kept the girls in stitches laughing at his silly jokes and imitations of famous people's voices. Ruth was drawn to his easygoing manner and creative sense of humor.

In the weeks that followed, Rachel babysat for Suzy several times, and eventually Toby suggested to Ruth that they all go to an amusement park together, his treat, as a special way of saying thank you. This led to a reciprocal dinner invitation for Indian cuisine at Ruth's place, followed by a couple of low key dates, and then to more time together as a group. It felt natural, it felt family, and it worked. For the first time in Ruth's life, she felt

85

like she had found a man who actually cared about her as a person rather than for what she could do for him. Toby was interested in what she liked, and asked her opinion about things, rather than telling her what to do or think. It was respect that he gave her, and she reveled in it.

Over time, the feelings between Ruth and Toby grew stronger, until he eventually asked Ruth to quit her job, which she did. This led to a small wedding before Ruth and her kids moved into Toby's house in the suburbs. It was a tight fit for the family of six in a small three-bedroom bungalow, but it was a healthy, stable home. Ruth learned to drive, and got an old Chrysler LeBaron so she could try to find work that is more dignified. She was able to leverage her cocktail experience to get hired as an early-shift Maitre D' at a high end restaurant a couple of miles away. The car, though, was her new baby, representing freedom of movement and not being a slave to bus schedules. The car represented upward mobility and having a better life for her and the girls. To most people the car would not be anything special, but to Ruth it was a Ferrari. She babied it, hand washed and waxed it and kept it immaculate. The car became an extension of herself and she accessorized it in every way possible, just the way a sixteen-year-old would with her first car – right down to the green fuzzy dice hanging from the rearview mirror.

Chapter 17

TIME: "Now"

"Rachel, could you help me set the table please. I have to help Suzy with her hair," Ruth asked.

"Sure, mom," said Rachel trying to act nonchalant. As challenging as Ruth's life had been she had always wanted better for her girls. Some might find it difficult to believe that a woman with Ruth's background and lack of intellectual prowess would provide strong encouragement to her daughters to succeed. Ruth knew those most successful in life had college degrees and she had met people who had come from circumstances worse than her own who had found ways to get through school and get good careers. Her marriage to Toby had reinforced that belief since he was a college graduate himself. Even when she worked at the club, Ruth always made the girls do their homework before she left for work. She tied rewards and privileges to A's and B's on their report cards and they had gotten the message as all of them were perennial honor students. One of the advantages of working nights was Ruth's ability to make her presence known at the girls' schools and she never missed a parent-teacher conference.

Rachel did not know how to talk to her mother about her pregnancy. Ruth would be crushed because she had always set the bar so high where school was concerned so for the time being, Rachel just put it out of her mind and focused on helping in the kitchen.

"Honey, I'm home! And I've got a surprise for you!" Toby yelled out as he crossed the threshold. Rachel peeked out of the kitchen at her dad and saw Uncle Ralph. "Uncle Ralph!" she yelled running over to give him a huge hug. "Great to see you," as she held him all her fears melted away for a moment and she was just left with a sense of peace that she had been lacking.

"Hey there Sweetie!" Ralph said, "You look wonderful and I can't believe how you've grown."

87

Rachel hadn't seen him since high school and had only seen him a handful of times since her parents wedding but each time his presence always had a calm, soothing effect on her. She loved the old man, even if he was somewhat mysterious with all his comings and goings. Rachel wasn't sure if her folks actually knew how to get hold of him but whenever he showed up he was always welcomed. He was a religious man who always insisted on saying grace before meals but he wasn't pushy or preachy. He was a person of faith so you watched your language around him out of respect. He was cool and the last person Rachel would ever imagine disrespecting.

"Ralph, you wonderful man how are you?" Ruth called out from the bedroom as she came out to greet her guest. "You will be staying for dinner," she insisted as she pulled up the extra chair from the desk and placed it at the table.

"How can I refuse?" He smiled.

"Ralph would you like to say grace for us?" Ruth offered.

They never did this unless they had a guest who did. The only one in the family who had any religious inkling at all was Maggie who had recently begun attending a youth group at a local parish.

"Sure, let's all hold hands," Ralph suggested as he prayed a beautiful prayer of thanksgiving for them. The family had a fun evening catching up with their trusted friend and benefactor. There were stories and laughs to go along with Ruth's signature dish and for a while, Rachel was able to lose herself in the merriment and ignore the fact that she was with child.

After dinner and a little more visiting Ralph excused himself and said he was going to 'get a move on', Rachel too excused herself saying that she needed some air and followed him out.

"You were much quieter than I remember you being Rachel, is there anything you care to talk about? You know I can keep a secret," he smiled.

"Oh, I'm sorry Uncle Ralph, it's just girl trouble nothing you could help with," Rachel answered.

"Well you're probably right then since I don't know much about 'girl troubles' personally," he admitted with a tiny hint of sarcasm in his voice. "But I know two women who do, and one of them is your mother. Whatever it is you're dealing with, she can probably relate to – remember her life hasn't always been as stable as it is now."

Rachel knew very little about her mother's background as Ruth rarely spoke about her childhood in foster care. Rachel remembered the early years when her mother had made bad decisions, which disrupted their lives almost constantly. For some reason though it was hard for Rachel to think of her mother as someone her age since she had always been a firm disciplinarian. Although many kids these days related to their parents on a more egalitarian model, Ruth had always put her foot down with her girls and kept a firm hand in everything the girls did. Rachel trusted her mother implicitly, and yet the idea of disappointing her when she had pined so much of her hopes on Rachel graduating and being a success was for the moment unbearable.

"The other one is the Virgin Mary," Ralph continued, "I figure an unplanned pregnancy by someone who had never even been with a man, in a time when women themselves were viewed as property and were stoned to death for being pregnant outside of wedlock qualifies her as someone who knows about 'girl troubles.' The only thing she had to go on was a promise from an angel that God was in charge. Whatever it is that you're dealing with, if you just keep her example in mind, her trusting God despite not being able to see how a difficult situation would all play out in the end, if you can just trust in Him like she did, you will be fine."

Ralph was staring at her right in the eye as he said it. Rachel thought she caught the shadow of her face's reflection in his iris.

"Ask Mary to pray with you to her Son for guidance and for faith – try it – what've you got to lose?" he smiled breaking the

89

intensity of the moment. Ralph could always talk about religion without it sounding contrived or preachy. Rachel didn't really get it but she did really like Ralph and appreciated his genuine concern.

"I don't have any of my cards on me; Oh here's an old card from a friend of mine. Let me give you my new cell phone number on the back of it. I know it looks kind of cheesy to be handwritten on someone else's card like that but it's all I've got," he said quickly penning his contact info on the back of someone else's business card. His handwriting was perfectly legible; it was like calligraphy. *Ralph St. Ange* was written with a cell phone number and an e-mail address underneath it.

"Call me if you do decide you want to talk," Ralph said as he gave her a paternal kiss on the forehead and departed. Rachel mechanically stuffed the card in her shoulder bag and quickly forgot about it.

Chapter 18

TIME: "Not-Now"

"How is she Doc? How's my baby?" Tom asked anxiously, his stomach was a bundle of nerves and his head was pounding from the fear and stress. The doctor looked somber, yet his poker face revealed nothing as he walked out of the ICU and removed the paper mask covering his mouth.

"She's stable," he replied, "but the way she came to the ground … well, it was a hard hit on her skull, three ribs are broken and her left knee is completely shattered – she's not out of the woods yet, the next few hours will be critical. She's in a coma right now. I thought it would be good for you and your wife to be with her. Over the years I've seen the presence of family members sometimes make an important difference in comatose patients' recoveries."

"Is there anything else we can do, donate blood, an organ, something?" Tom asked.

"Just pray. I've seen prayer do wonders. I can't really explain it scientifically but I can appreciate the results I've seen during my career with people praying. Go be with your daughter, she needs you," the doctor ordered.

Tom, Rachel, and Elijah went into the room.

"Oh my baby!" wailed Rachel as she approached her daughter's bed. They couldn't really recognize Rita except for the sign that said 'Pierce' in black magic marker on a two inch piece of masking tape that had been placed on the wall by the head of the bed. Rita was covered from head to toe in machines, tubes, wires, casts and all of that was encapsulated inside a plastic bubble. The machines beeped and whirred around her. There were two flimsy plastic chairs in the corner of the room, which Tom retrieved, and placed by the bedside. He took Elijah on his lap as Rachel mourned her child's health.

91

"Baby, I'm so sorry," Rachel cried. "Why did this happen to you? Why didn't this happen to me instead. Oh God! I'd do anything to trade places with you baby, anything!"

Rachel pondered the Old Testament story of King David, and how God punished him for his adultery with Bathsheba by killing their first child ... she wondered if this was to be her punishment as well for the many sins she had committed, for how close she had come to aborting Rita. Rachel just put her hands on the plastic tent that surrounded her daughter, it was as close as she could come to touching her and out of habitual deference to her agnostic husband, she prayed silently.

"Daddy?" Elijah's boy soprano voice squeaked timidly.

"Yes Eli?" Tom replied softly.

"Is that Rita in there?" she was so covered in tubes and devices that her little brother did not recognize her.

Tom just broke down completely, "Yes son, it is. She is very, very sick and needs us to be here for her." Elijah, a normally spry lad was overcome with the gravity of the situation and was behaving abnormally calm and serious.

Later that night, when both Eli and Rachel were passed out in the chairs, Tom was totally transfixed by the sight of his daughter and could not look away from her.

"Oh Rita, honey, I'm so sorry this happened. It's all my fault; if I had just been more responsible and not so lazy we could have gone to the park to play. Oh sweetie, what Daddy wouldn't give to trade places with you," Tom said.

"Would you give up your pride, Tom?" said an unknown man's voice behind him. Startled out of his sorrow, Tom turned to see a nicely dressed older man.

"My name is Ralph; I'm a longtime family friend. I've heard a lot about you Tom. I'm glad to finally get a chance to meet you

92

though I wish it were under better circumstances," he said not offering his hand.

"I'll wake Rachel for you," Tom replied.

"No, don't bother her. Please let her rest." Ralph said somberly.

"So what did you mean about my pride?" Tom asked.

"Tom, you've seen God work all around you for many years. He helped you to get your wife, helped you have a family, He's been there in all of your trials and tribulations and He's always given you the means to overcome your worst fears and circumstances," Ralph said. "He has shown you His love by transforming Rachel from a self-centered girlfriend to a loving wife. He has blessed you with a brilliant daughter who has the potential to do absolutely amazing things and a great son who He has plans for as well but He wants something more Tom. He's looking for the whole family to join to him and that includes you."

"Look Ralph, my personal business is none of your concern," Tom retorted.

"A minute ago you were admitting fault for Rita being in this condition, I'm just working with that," Ralph replied.

Tom just sat there without moving as tears ran silently down his face.

"Listen to me Tom. Many people don't get all the gifts that you've gotten in life and in love. You work hard and you are a good man but your intellectual pride is holding you back from asking God to take charge of this situation. Look at your daughter, she's hurt and needs help, the kind of help you can't give," Ralph explained. "This is a situation that intellect cannot control, you're a smart man, you should be able to see that – but just in case you can't – I'm here telling it to you. Your intellect can't fix Rita, her problem is bigger than you, and you need the help of someone bigger than this situation. You need Jesus Christ and

93

He is ready and waiting for you to ask for His help. However, it's up to you. Therefore, I repeat my initial question. To heal your daughter would you give up your pride?" he asked firmly, his tone not wavering.

"I would do anything to have Rita whole again," Tom insisted.

"Then Tom, why don't you lead us in a prayer for her health," Ralph suggested.

"Sure, why not? It's the only thing I haven't tried." Tom replied. "Dear God, I've suspected You were there all along and I've ignored You because if You weren't real then that meant that I could do things my way. But my way can't help Rita right now so I am willing to try it Your way because I believe that You are bigger than this situation and at this point You are my only hope to heal her. Amen." Tom prayed this prayer then broke down again. This time Ralph knelt down, embraced Tom, and let him cry.

"That was an honest prayer Tom and I know God is pleased and I believe that He will answer it the way you want Him too. Although I'm warning you for future reference, sometimes the answer is 'No.' Turn around, I think she's waking up," Ralph said.

"Rita!" Tom's ecstatic cry woke Rachel and they both ran over to see Rita's eyes open slowly; they were so excited that they did not see Ralph quietly leave.

Chapter 19

TIME: "Now"

Rachel waved goodbye as Ralph drove away. She wanted a little privacy so she got in her car through the passenger side door, which worked better than the driver's side, got behind the wheel, and drove over to the Wal-Mart parking lot a couple of miles away. In contrast to the heat of the day, it was a comfortable evening. One side of the Wal-Mart backed up to a river that ran through the city and on the other side you could see the downtown lights shining over the water at night. Young people referred to this area as the 'Redneck Riviera.' They would park on this side to make out, hang around in their cars, and listen to music. Every now and then, a police car would cruise by; if there were not a lot of people loitering, the police would usually just ignore them. Unknown to the local youth, the sheriff's patrol monitored which license plates were there regularly – they figured it was better for the kids to be some place where they could keep tabs on them as long as there weren't any fights. Rachel wanted to just sit and enjoy the evening and listen to some music but as she did, she started crying, sobbing and yelling as it all came out – it needed to.

No, she thought, *I'll just go inside and get a coffee at the snack bar, it was only one dollar there.* Then she remembered that she still didn't have any money on her and that made all her feelings gush forth again.

Well, she was going to have to talk to Tom. Funny how she had wanted him there when she was going in to the clinic but since making the follow-up appointment, she was considerably less enthusiastic about talking to him. She needed to though since Tom would be paying for the abortion, as she didn't have the money. The only thing she had of any value in the world was her lousy Chrysler LeBaron and it had been a high school graduation present from her parents – a sort of hand me down from her mother.

Rachel took her cell phone and pushed the number 'two' for a long second, enough to activate the pre-programmed speed dial

95

for Tom's cell phone number. Number 'two' had a long history of being the generic speed dial button for the main man in her life. Each time she dated a new guy his name would replace the old name under the number 'two' speed dial. Rachel explained to her girlfriends on campus that the guy would always be number 'two' because he had better make sure she felt like number one – number two was the most a man could ever hope to be with her – it always got a giggle from the girls.

The phone rang three times and then Tom picked it up. "Hey babe I'm right in the middle of kicking Richard's butt in War craft..." Tom lived in an apartment off campus with a super dorky roommate named Richard. The two of them were constantly playing those stupid video games like little kids and Rachel hated video games. Rachel hated anything that distracted a man's attention when she wanted it.

"Hey Tom, we need to talk," Rachel replied.

"I'm all ears babe!" Tom replied, clearly distracted by all the fake explosions Rachel heard in the background. It sounded like Richard was shouting and cheering too.

"No Tom, this is serious, I need to see you, I'm over at the Riviera about to go in for a coffee, but I'll wait for you."

"I'll be there in five minutes!" Tom replied. He was scared. Rachel was seldom to the point when she spoke. Whatever it was – was big ... *could she be breaking up with me,* he thought? A tight knot formed in the pit of Tom's stomach as he let his worst fears overcome him. *Did she meet someone else? Maybe an old boyfriend she was still friendly with had come back into the picture? Was he going to lose the first real girlfriend he had ever had?* He slapped on his best cologne – the ridiculously expensive one she said she really liked, grabbed his car keys, and headed out the door with a hundred different scenarios dancing in his head.

Tom dated in high school and college, had even spent the night with women a couple of times but nothing had ever lasted. It wasn't for lack of effort as Tom had always wanted a relationship for as long as he could remember. What seemed to come naturally to some people was like pulling teeth to him. Tom was in love with Rachel but also in love with the feeling of loving someone. He could not believe such a beautiful woman had gone out with him more than once. Tom was a classic nerd, very smart, with a keen, scientific mind, and he was a math whiz. He had limited social skills and no taste in clothing. However, he was changing these things now because of Rachel, who had started teaching him what to wear and how to style his hair, and had encouraged him to use deodorant more frequently. She also taught him how to communicate with people. He was learning what to say, when to just be quiet and listen. She was helping him to develop these missing skills and he appreciated it.

Tom's bookish personality was the exact opposite of Rachel's. She was the quintessential social butterfly, very perceptive and very sensitive to contemporary etiquette, fashion, and protocol. Rachel's friends constantly teased her about Tom, referring to them as the 'odd couple.' Most of them would not have given Tom the time of day if he were not dating their friend.

They met at a campus party in which alcohol played a major role. Rachel was just dumped by a boyfriend, and alcohol was her main choice of comfort. By the time she encountered Tom, she had already participated in more than one 'keg stand,' and had not turned down any other glass that had been offered. Tom had also had a couple of beers to loosen him up so that he could approach girls more fearlessly. That night he had been wearing his 'lucky clothes': his one outfit that was almost stylish and might even be considered fairly 'cool,' particularly when the lighting was bad. They danced a couple of times, then slow danced, and started kissing even before they knew each other's names. A quick, alcohol-induced conversation, which neither of them remembered, led to her coming home with him that night.

The morning brought both shock and an excruciating headache for Rachel – shock at the 'geek' she was lying next to, and a headache of the worst kind as her body punished her for being dehydrated from all the alcohol she drank. She also felt wrenchingly sick. He spent the rest of the next day babying her, cooking for her, massaging her head, looking after her as her face periodically changed color, cleaning up after her numerous near-encounters with the porcelain deity she had to bow before, and just showing genuine concern. She had been impressed enough to spend more time with him and to want to get to know him better.

Tom came from a normal family. His parents were successful professionals and moderate churchgoers – so moderate, in fact, that he had just never really understood the benefit of going. As soon as he was old enough to stay home without them having to get a babysitter, he quit going to church, and they let him. One Christmas they asked him to come along and when he asked why he should, they could not come up with a good reason, so they never asked again.

With Rachel, Tom was actually dating someone steady, for the first time. He enjoyed calling Rachel, 'Honey,' and she didn't seem to mind. She was teaching him how to interact in a social atmosphere along with other social graces he lacked. In return, Tom showed Rachel what it was like to have someone care for her without expecting something in return.

Rachel had been to the doctor's today, which caused Tom to think about different scenarios. *Oh my God!* he thought, *she must have VD! That's why she didn't want to talk over the phone. Oh God, I hope it's not AIDS!* Now his mind was racing a mile a minute. An unfortunate side effect of his brilliance was that Tom could really race ahead to the worst possible scenario and scare himself into or out of doing something long before anything ever happened. *What if she has AIDS!?* he worried. She had been around quite a bit more than he had, so there was always a risk.

The first time they had gotten together, he had worn a condom, but after that, since he knew she was on the pill, he didn't think of still having to use condoms. Besides, even if they were effective against AIDS, they weren't foolproof so why bother? The fact was, he was so into Rachel that at the time he didn't care. And it wasn't until they had been together for a couple of months that he learned the depth of her sexual history, but by then he was committed. Now he was worried that that had been

98

the absolute wrong decision, and he hoped it wasn't any of that. *Please, God, don't let it be AIDS!* he prayed. When people are faced with desperate circumstances of life or death situations, atheism goes right out the proverbial window.

Tom pulled up next to Rachel in his chrome black flair-side Chevrolet extended cab pickup, a graduation present from his parents three years earlier, which he kept very clean. It had leather seats and a top-of-the-line stereo with Jensen speakers that might have been able to blow the windows out if they were ever cranked up all the way. He had a sprayed-on rhino bed liner and put a shiny chrome toolbox on the back. Tom might not have been very cool, but his truck sure was. It had gotten him more than one date in past situations where his personality was not up to par.

Tom's social life had really started changing in the last year. The summer before his junior year, he made friends with a classmate who was very socially adept and excellent at finding ways to approach women and start a conversation. The guy was also flat broke and had no wheels of his own. Tom would do the driving while his friend would converse with the girls – a strategy that worked as long as Tom remained relatively quiet. His social awkwardness was like a radar beacon that would sometimes scare off the girls.

"What's up? Does it have to do with your doctor's visit today?" Tom asked nervously, trying to seem cool, but really unable to hide his anxiety.

Trying hard to stifle a laugh, Rachel noted that Tom was wearing a weird pink shirt with an alligator on it. The cut was wrong and the buttons were on the wrong side – any other fool could see that it was a woman's shirt. He must have found it at Goodwill. *What a nerd! How could I have let myself get involved with this dork?* Rachel wondered.

"Yes," she replied seriously, looking him straight in the eye. Tom's heart sunk, his face flushed two shades warmer than his pink shirt, his temperature rose, and his nerves were just about at the breaking point as he hung on her every word.

"Tom, I'm pregnant." Rachel said without emotion.

A huge wave of relief swept over him before the implications of this new reality set in.

"Whew! Oh honey, I was so afraid it would be something much worse," Tom jabbered quickly.

"Really? What could be worse than this?" Rachel had never thought seriously about there being anything worse much than this. His reaction caught her off guard.

"Oh honey, the way you sounded, I was afraid you were going to tell me you had some horrible diagnosis from the doctor. So you're pregnant? Well, that's not so bad," he smiled. "It's not the order I thought things would happen in, but now you kind of have to marry me, right?"

"What?" she said incredulously. "You're not serious, are you?"

"I'm very serious; in fact I've never been more serious. You know that I love you, and we've talked before about the future, and I've told you that I just don't see a future without you in it," Tom said excitedly. "To me, this just moves the timetable forward a little bit. How far a long are you?"

"Six weeks," Rachel replied numbly.

"Okay, so a month and a half out of nine. This is November. That means she was conceived in early October, so the baby should be coming in June. I graduate in May, so the timing will work out just fine," he said cheerily. "This is exciting! *Having my baby ...*" he started singing a silly rendition of an old Paul Anka tune, grabbing both of her hands in his as if they were a microphone.

"You're ridiculous!" Rachel said, pulling away. "How can you joke at a time like this? You're graduating, but I still have two more years after this one, if and only if I'm able to finish next semester. I can't afford to be pregnant right now. No, Tom, it's a bad idea. I can't have this baby right now," and she proceeded to list all the reasons she had written on one side of the piece of paper in Candy's office earlier – except the ones that had something to do with him rejecting the child or rejecting her, because clearly that would not be the case here.

"Well, let's go inside and get a coffee and talk about this some more – and you should probably just have a juice," he said, giving her a sweet little kiss on the forehead and leading her inside Wal-mart.

Tom bought Rachel an orange juice and got himself a cup of coffee before joining her at one of the plastic picnic tables in the snack bar. Rachel really couldn't fathom Tom's reaction. *Didn't he get it?* This was not at all what she was expecting. *Maybe he wasn't as smart as his 3.9 grade point average in mechanical engineering implied.* Plus, he was being such a dork singing little songs and acting all happy at this terrible news. Rachel was a B-minus student and she was studying softer classes. Technically, she was supposed to be a Psych major, but so far, she had been focusing on getting her general education requirements completed so that then she could take the classes that really interested her rather than the ones that she cared nothing about and barely held her attention. Her performance academically thus far had been sub-par for her mother's expectations.

"Rachel, honey, think of this baby as a reflection of all the best of you and all the best of me put together. If it's a little boy maybe we can call him 'junior.' I've always thought that would be cool to have a 'Tom Junior.' If it's a girl, she'll look just like you. Wouldn't that be wonderful?" Tom asked.

"Stop it, Tom! I'm serious! Have you listened to anything that I've said? Apparently not. Let me make it clear to you. I DO NOT WANT TO BE PREGNANT," she exclaimed through clenched teeth. "I think you're a great guy, you have a lot to offer, and you are really sweet, but I DO NOT WANT TO MARRY YOU. I'm

101

only twenty years old, I have my whole life ahead of me, and I don't want to get stuck with a bunch of kids the way my mother did. What I want from you is very straightforward. I need $600 to get this taken care of as fast as possible."

Tom was devastated. He knew that she wasn't in love with him, but he hoped in time that would change. She had never said that she was, and she had never really said much whenever he had broached the subject of their prospects for being together in the long term. Even though he had known it, it still tore right through him to hear it from her. She did not want to marry him. In Tom's mind, this was his dream girl, and the idea of her being with someone else was unthinkable. Tom was beyond smitten – he was hopelessly devoted to her; to him, in his mind, the logical course of action would be for them to get married. This child could be the tie that bound them together forever, so he had some serious sales work to do. Fortunately, he knew she didn't have any money, and was pretty sure her mother wouldn't lend it to her for that purpose even if she had it, which he doubted. So he had that part going for him. Trying to maintain an appearance of not being heartbroken, and hoping that the lump in his throat didn't give him away, Tom started his best effort at the hard sell. "Rachel, I know that I'm not like the other guys that you've been with. I'm not cool; I'm just a nerd..."

"Look, Tom, I didn't mean to be so blunt, but..." she interrupted.

"Babe, be quiet for a second," Tom continued. "I know I don't fit in with your friends, and I know that right now you're not in love with me, but I know you know how I feel about you. And I want nothing more than to make a life with you. I may be able to provide for us just in time for when the baby is born, and I don't think that's a coincidence. I think it's fate. I think we are meant to be, and I want to make sure that you know that I am in this for the long haul. This baby, it's my baby too. I know you think of me as being immature, and I guess in some ways I am – maybe I don't have all the experience with relationships and the opposite sex as you do, but I'm ready for this. I will be a good husband for you, and I will be a good father for junior. I want this, and I want you," he said, staring at her straight in the eye, transfixing her with the intensity of his gaze.

"Dang you, Tom, you're not making this easy!" she said, shaking her head and rolling it around to avoid his mesmerizing stare.

"This is our big chance, Rachel. We messed up somehow, but we can fix it," Tom said.

"No, Tom, I messed up. I forgot my pill three days in a row during mid-terms, and each one of those nights I was at your apartment," Rachel said, not really looking at Tom but staring off into space.

"But we can come out of this situation stronger and with more than we went into it with," Tom pleaded. "I know one thing, Rachel, and that's this: you will never find anyone who loves you as much as I do, and I love the idea of our baby ..."

"You gotta stop talking that way, Tom. There is no 'our baby.' I am pregnant and now I am going to be un-pregnant next Saturday. I've already made the appointment. I just need the $600," Rachel said sternly.

"Un-pregnant? I've never heard that word before. Now who's not being serious? Rachel, having an abortion doesn't make you 'un-pregnant'; it just makes you the mother of a dead baby!" Tom retorted.

That last admonition felt like a slap across the face to Rachel.

"SCREW YOU!" she fired back as she threw the rest of her orange juice at him and ran out of the snack bar, down the aisle, and out into the Wal-mart parking lot without looking back.

Hurt and covered in sticky orange juice, Tom grabbed a hunk of napkins out of the metal dispenser on the table and started wiping himself off. He ignored his first inclination to go running after her. *No,* he thought, *let her stew for awhile. I'll call her tomorrow night. I still have a week before her appointment, and she still doesn't have any money, so I may get a little more time.*

III. The Choice

Chapter 20

Rachel felt so drained. Nothing in her life was going right – the pregnancy, the abortion, the money, the boyfriend, all of it – all wrong. The one thing she needed right now she couldn't have – privacy, alone time, the chance to decompress and figure things out. Walking into the house, she knew her sisters would be checking their Instagram and Facebook accounts on the computer, so she just went straight to bed. Her room was the second largest of the three bedrooms, and she shared it with Maggie. They each had a bed and a dresser of their own. None of the furniture matched but they didn't care, because they knew they were lucky to have what they did. Things had been worse a few years ago – much worse, and on many different levels.

"Hey, Sissy, what're you doing home on a Saturday night? I don't remember the last time this happened." Maggie was a couple of years younger than her sister and she wasn't considered terribly attractive or outgoing, so she usually didn't go out a lot. Her social life had increased exponentially though of late, due to the church youth group she had started attending. Now she had things to go to every Sunday and Wednesday night, and was getting invited out to parties and outings by her new friends. Maggie was a shy girl and, unlike Rachel, her physical appearance alone would never win her much positive attention. Rachel was happy that her sister was finally getting a life, even if she didn't understand the church part of it. Maggie was right, Rachel was hardly ever home on a weekend night and if not for her current state of mind, she would have been out all night.

"I'm really beat, Mags. I just want to put my pajamas on and turn in."

"Since you're home early tonight, I don't suppose you'd want to come to church with me tomorrow?" Maggie asked hopefully.

"Mags ..." Rachel said in a tone of voice that indicated that asking that question was a mistake.

"Ok, Ok. Can't blame a girl for trying. Well, I'll turn the light out and go wait my turn at the computer. Get some rest, Sissy!" Finally, Rachel was alone. She just let her mind drift ... baby ... marriage ... no ....

Chapter 21

TIME: "Not-Now"

Such a proud moment! I can't believe it! My baby's getting her MD and she's barely old enough to drive! Tom thought. What an unbelievable day! At a time when most kids are thinking about the junior prom, Rita was graduating from medical school. Receiving offers from prestigious medical institutions all over the country was a luxury many young doctors don't get. Since Rita was so young, her parents arranged her residency at the local Catholic Hospital. Tom had his doubts about his daughter actually practicing medicine. She had shown great promise as a researcher, where her interest was in discovering the unknown. She had already published a couple of papers on immunology and was really fascinated by retroviral research. She would probably end up either at a well-funded government facility with access to cutting edge technology, or at a research department of a drug company with deep pockets. For the time being, though, Rita would live at home and learn about the general practice of medicine at the hospital.

"Smile, Rita," Rachel said as she took a picture of her little girl in her cap and gown making a silly face at her two little brothers. "All I'm asking for is one picture with a smile."

106

Chapter 22

TIME: "Now"

The week had been tough. Rachel had not taken any of Tom's calls, but instead made herself scarce between classes, rather than meeting up with Tom. She had succeeded in avoiding him completely since throwing the orange juice at him. On Monday and Tuesday, he had tried several times to reach her by phone, by e-mail, and on Facebook. On Wednesday, he tried only once. On Thursday he gave up, which was very unexpected. Rachel figured he had finally gotten the message that she was going to follow through with her plan to abort and was just sulking about it. The biggest disappointment was that Tom wouldn't be paying for the abortion, so Rachel needed to seek other alternatives for the money.

Rachel put the finishing touches on her 'negotiation outfit.' She had used her best make-up and left her hair flowing down her shoulders. She was wearing a very short black skirt that emphasized the curvature of her hips, and sheer pantyhose that really gave her legs a smooth look without an artificial sheen. Her neckline plunged down, which she accessorized with a little blue dichroic glass chocker design that set off the entire package. She topped if off with heels, figuring that if she was dealing with men, she would surely do well with this look.

"First stop is the pawn shop," Rachel said out loud as she pulled into the familiar looking parking lot of the old building with bars on the windows and door. She got out through the passenger side door and grabbed the box with her china doll and the ornate silver Mother-Daughter, double-hearted locket her mother had given her when she was a little girl. She had removed the little cutout pictures of her and her mother that had been in it the night before. She would save those, but she was desperate, and the locket needed to go.

"Good morning," the chipper girl with thick, nerdy-looking glasses behind the counter said as Rachel opened the door. A door alarm made a pleasant chirping noise to indicate that it had been opened. The girl had a bright green name tag on that said,

107

'Julia.' She was wearing an awful plaid jumper that looked home-made, a big cross around her neck, and enormous, thick, horn-rimmed glasses that had to have been antique. Rachel figured she must be home-schooled. *Dang!* She was hoping it'd be a man whom she could manipulate.

"Have you got some good stuff for us today?" she asked sweetly.

"This is as good as I have," Rachel replied, placing the box on the glass counter between them.

"For a loan or for sale?" the girl inquired.

"For sale," Rachel replied sadly, removing her prized possession from the tissue paper inside the box. "This is a very special doll. Her name is Rita. She was the second one I ever got when I was little after some kids on the playground tore up my rag doll. Isn't she beautiful? She means more to me than anything in the world. I've given my heart to her so many times that I feel like she's a real person with a full personality. We've spent countless hours together playing house and tea party and – oh listen to me, I'm being so silly." Rachel was trying to swallow through the lump that was forming in her throat. "It's just a doll," she said fighting back the tears.

"Wow, yes, that's real porcelain from Europe, isn't it? Hand painted. And that dress – it's gorgeous!" Julia said.

"I've always taken really good care of this. It's killing me to have to do this, but I'm desperate. What can you give me for her?"

"Gosh, I'm sorry. It is beautiful and you've taken such good care of it. Unfortunately, there's not a lot of demand for things like this. I would have a hard time re-selling it. I could probably give you $30," Julia replied.

"What about this locket?" Rachel asked, handing over her other treasure.

"It looks like real silver, and the price of silver is as high as it's ever been, so I could probably get you $30 for this. That'd be $60 for both," Julia said.

"I have no choice. Can I at least get a couple of cold cokes from the cooler?" Rachel asked as she handed over the doll that she had thought of as her own child for most of her life and the special Mother-Daughter silver locket that her mom had given her.

"Sure, help yourself. The door is unlocked," the sales girl said, writing up the bill of sale.

That was a lot harder than I thought it would be, Rachel said to herself as she drove away from the pawnshop. She was still amazed at herself that she was able to let go of the two things she loved most in the world – things that were more like parts of her than mere objects. She decided that it must be a sign of maturity, and turned the radio a little louder so that she wouldn't have to feel herself mourn.

109

Chapter 23

TIME: "Not-Now"

"So is our famous daughter coming home this weekend?" Tom asked as Rachel got off the phone and walked into the living room.

"Yes and she says she's got some big news for us." Rachel replied mysteriously.

"I don't suppose it's another award for discovering some new retroviral therapy? Let me guess, she got her name on another new patent right ...?" Tom asked again.

"It sounded more personal. I'm thinking it has to do with that fellow she's been dating since she's bringing him too." Rachel replied.

"Oh for crying out loud, she's only known him a little while you don't suppose ...." Tom started to say.

"Take your overly-protective father hat off for a second and think about it. Our baby is twenty-five years old, has a great career, and makes more than both of us combined." Rachel reminded him.

"I know, I know. It's just that, aw heck, it's just hard to think of her all grown up like this, bringing some guy home," he said glumly.

"I'm sure he'll be great." Rachel said "C'mon sour puss it's time to wake the triplets from their nap. The older boys will be home soon and you promised to take us all out to Chuck-e-Cheese for pizza tonight."

Chapter 24

TIME: "Now"

"Next stop, 'Tote the note'", Rachel said aloud. 'Tote the note' was a used car dealership where people with very little money and no credit would buy vehicles that barely ran for a few hundred dollars down and make payments on it each pay check until it was paid off or stopped running. It was called, 'Tote the note' because the dealership would hold the title to the car until all the payments were made even though the buyer would get actual possession of it. Oftentimes the vehicles would breakdown and the drivers would stop making payments so the dealership would repossess them, fix them, and sell them again. Rachel pulled into the lot, past the barbed wire fence towards what looked like the office, just a little temporary building that had been nicely painted, with multicolored flags strewn out from the roof to other places on the property. A giant inflatable monkey was on the roof. The sound of guard dogs barking not too far away made her wince, as she was deathly afraid of big dogs.

"It's a piece of garbage!" Honest Abe said. "I can't sell this."

"It runs." Rachel replied. "Anytime you can get a car that runs for $1000 it's a good deal. Go ahead, look under the hood."

"Honest Abe," the owner of the used car dealership opened up the door to a huge screech. "You're not serious!" he exclaimed, reaching for the lever to pop the hood and pulling it before slamming the door shut and walking around to the front of the car.

"The motor alone is worth $1000." she said.

"I don't think so" Honest Abe replied, "these things are not exactly in demand for parts, friggin' Chryslers don't last more than five years, and this thing is a dinosaur."

111

"It's not new, but if it were then I wouldn't be here at, 'Tote the Note.' I'd be over at a real dealership trading it in," she replied sourly.

"Listen, I can't give you what you want for it but why don't you let me sell it for you on consignment. Many of my customers are farm laborers and they aren't picky about things. I could probably sell this to my immigrant clients on consignment if you split it with me."

"Sorry, no deal. I need cash today; if I can't do it here then I'll try the guy down the street at 'Harry who Carries.' Did I mention that the air conditioning works?" Rachel replied sarcastically.

"Hey wait, you didn't say that the AC works, let me check it out," he said opening the car door back up to another loud screech and turning on the AC. "Hey, that's not bad, the migrant workers aren't used to air conditioning. It's kind of a status symbol for them. I could probably get $500 for this which means you'd have to sell it to me for $250."

"Sir, I'm sorry. I'm in a bind. I can't play this game because I need an operation and I gotta have the money today. It's gonna cost me $750 so that's my drop dead price, on top of that I need a ride to the doctor's office." Rachel started crying to emphasize the gravity of the situation.

"An operation, you look so good though … listen kid … I'm an old softie at heart and you're such a pretty girl, I can't stand to see you suffer. I'll give you $650 and a ride to the doctor and that's the best I can do," he said with a deeply sympathetic tone.

"At $700 I'll be able to get a taxi ride home after the operation," Rachel implored.

"At $675 you don't have to tip the driver, did you bring the title?" Honest Abe asked holding out his hand to close the deal.

"Yes, of course," she said reaching out to shake his hand.

After she signed the title over to him in exchange for the cash, he said, "Now for that ride, let's take my car. Hey Pedro! You're in charge while I give this lady a ride!" he called out to a guy who started working on the busted door to what used to be Rachel's LeBaron.

Rachel got in the passenger side of his car, it was nice – a nearly new black Maxima, much better than anything else on his lot with a Florida vanity plate that said, 'totus tuus', which she figured meant something in Spanish. She noted the nicely upholstered seats and all the buttons and dials on the dash and the console between them. *This car was loaded and so clean,* she thought. She took note of the bright-multicolored little statue on the dashboard. "What's this? I've never seen this figure before, it looks kind of mysterious?" Rachel said.

"That, my dear, is Our Lady of Guadalupe, Queen of the Americas and Empress of Mexico." Abe replied.

"You don't look Mexican," she said making polite conversation. "I didn't know they had a queen over there."

"I'm not," Abe smiled, "but I am a Catholic and "Our Lady of Guadalupe" was an apparition of the Virgin Mary down in Mexico in the sixteen century. She appeared to a humble Indian peasant we now call Saint Juan Diego. She told him to tell the Bishop to build a church in a particular spot. The Bishop didn't believe him so he asked for impossible proof that it was true. The Bishop told Juan Diego that if the Virgin Mary did appear to him then bring back a Castilian rose as a sign. Castilian roses didn't grow in Mexico and it was winter so the Bishop was really giving him an impossible task. Remember this is way before refrigeration and modern transportation. Well, Juan told Our Lady what the Bishop said and sure enough she made a bunch of roses appear and told him to collect them all in his cloak and bring them to the Bishop as proof, so he did. When Juan got to the Bishop and opened his cloak to show him the roses this exact image of Mary appeared on his cloak while the Bishop and two other men were watching. The cloak is kept in the Church that she had asked to be built down in Mexico and in the following ten years all the

113

Indians in Mexico were converted to Christianity and all of the human sacrifices that the Aztecs were performing stopped."

"Ok, so it's not a real Queen it's just a title for the Virgin Mary? I was confused. I didn't think there were any monarchs in the Americas. Well I learned something new, I never heard that the Aztecs practiced human sacrifice."

"That's because it's not very politically correct Miss. So it doesn't get a lot of attention in the modern history books. They like to focus a lot on positive cultural contributions of the Native Americans, which is all fine and good but it's only one side of the story. Our Lady of Guadalupe is also the patroness of the unborn; she's the one whose prayers will ultimately put an end to the slaughter of the innocent unborn through abortion. Just as her prayers ended the killing of the innocent in Mexico, so too will her prayers put an end to the horrible killings of innocent babies here in America." Abe said.

Rachel's face turned red and she began sweating. She couldn't believe what she was hearing; now she was upset. She was scared of her situation and uncomfortable being in the car with Honest Abe as her heart raced a mile a minute. Abe sensed her discomfort and figured she must be post-abortive.

Abe was a long time prayer warrior for life. While he no longer stood outside abortion clinics praying and counseling the way he had done it in his younger days, he still devoted a great deal of his personal prayer time to the subject and gave generously to the Catholic Charities Pregnancy Center.

"It's hot in here. Can you turn up the AC?" she squeaked.

"Sure, no problem, sorry for hitting you with all the religious stuff but you did ask," he reminded her.

"No worries Abe, is that a Satellite radio?" she asked changing the subject.

"Yes indeed, XM, what would you like to hear?" he asked nicely.

114

"How about some 80's music?" she suggested, and was delighted as he turned it on to the 80's station to hear the 'Safety Dance' – one of her all-time favorites that lightened her mood. "Thanks Honest Abe, I appreciate it."

"So where is this operation taking place? Over at a hospital or a doc-in-the- box?" he asked inquisitively.

"Neither, actually. It's a clinic over on Fester Street by the University," Rachel said as she fumbled in her purse for the address. "It's at 8686 Fester."

"Ok, I can get us there. I don't go that way much – it's the one part of town that's rougher than where my lot is," he said, laughing as they drove on for another ten minutes.

As they got up closer, Rachel said, "It's over there on the left where those people are standing."

Abe looked over and recognized a couple of people that he knew. Abe didn't stop. He just kept going straight and almost ran a red light.

"Hey, you missed it!!" Rachel yelled. "What the hell are you doing?"

"Nothing. The deal's off," he said, not slowing down for another yellow light.

"You're crazy! Let me out or I'm calling the police!" she screamed.

"You want to call the police, fine, use my phone. The number is 911. You can tell them to pick you up back at my lot. Have your lawyer there because mine will be too. You didn't tell me I would be driving you to an abortion clinic. I didn't recognize the address, but I saw two people who I know are pro-life sidewalk counselors out there, so I know what that place was. Since the drive was part of the deal and you withheld information from me that would have caused me to violate my deepest held religious

115

beliefs by facilitating an abortion, I believe you are in breach of contract. Your car sucks. I think the state lemon law gives me the right to return the vehicle to you for what I paid for it. I want my money back. In the meantime, enjoy the radio" Abe said.

Rachel was completely dumbfounded. She should have gone to the other place to sell her car; now it looked like that would be what she had to do.

"And just in case you're thinking you're going to try to sell your car to 'Larry who Carries,' he goes to my church too," Abe added.

Rachel was fuming mad. She wasn't sure if what he was saying was true or not, but she decided not to call the police, just in case what he claimed was correct. She didn't have the money for a lawyer either, so she really didn't feel like she could fight. She just started breaking down right there in his car, humiliated by her helplessness.

Abe started to pray aloud. "Heavenly Father, I don't know what circumstances this sister of mine is in, and I can only imagine the misfortunes she faces in her life, so I pray, Father, that You will bless her with every good thing, and show Your love and concern to her in every possible way. Please help her to see that no matter how dark the circumstances, You are right there with her, comforting and trying to guide her. Help her to see You and Your love in a new way this very day, and turn her heart away from herself and towards the child she carries in her womb. I pray in Jesus' holy name, through the intercession of Our Lady of Guadalupe, Amen."

When they got back to the lot, Abe let her out of the passenger side of the car as a sign of respect, and led her to the office, where he returned her keys and title and recovered his money.

"So, that's what you needed the operation for, huh? To have a baby removed? Listen, my wife and I have four children – all of them are adopted. We were never able to conceive on our own, and we just feel so blessed by the family we've been able to have because of the loving generosity of people like yourself. They found themselves in circumstances that seemed overwhelming but made the decision to lovingly place their babies with us rather than to kill them," Abe continued. "You seem like a decent person; you don't seem like the kind who would have any business paying somebody to dismember your baby when there are a long line of people who can't get babies and want them. Right now, you probably hate me, so I don't expect you to bless me with your child, although my wife and I would be willing to adopt her if you were open to discussing it."

"Please take this brochure," he said, reaching into his desk and pulling out a brochure from Catholic Charities entitled, ADOPTION THE LOVING OPTION. "Read through it. It has stories that you might be able to relate to in it, and has contact information for some wonderful people who can help you and your baby. I care, and I will be praying for you. You can call me if you want to talk or if you want me to put you in touch with my friends."

Rachel took the brochure and silently walked out to reclaim her car. She was pleasantly surprised to see that the driver's side door had been fixed while she'd been away; opening it without hearing that familiar loud rubbing noise was almost like getting a new car! She reached onto the dashboard, which had been rubbed down with shiny turtle wax, and removed the big handmade sign that said, "SE VENDE $2750," and tossed it on the ground. One final glance over at the little building showed Honest Abe on the phone – probably calling Larry to warn him about her.

Well, it wasn't a total loss, she thought as she got in and turned the ignition. Her car door was fixed and she had money for gas. Making a quick call to the abortion clinic to postpone her appointment for a week, she listened to Candy's warning that 'the price would go up.' Maybe she ought to take a ride to the beach. It would be too cold for a Florida native to go swimming, but she did like to be out by the water, park the car, and stare out at the horizon. It helped her to dream of more exciting places and possibilities for her life.

117

Chapter 25

TIME: "Not-Now"

The reporters were all over their yard like ants at a picnic. Rachel had shut the blinds in all the windows, and the police had finally arrived to control the crowd and get everyone off the property. This was the biggest medical breakthrough of the third millennium, and somehow word had gotten around that the famous Dr. Rita Pierce-Saured would be visiting her parents before heading over to Oslo to pick up the Nobel Prize for medicine. She had broken the genome of the common cold virus and developed a prototype anti-retroviral therapy that could destroy retroviruses, thus rendering the dreaded HIV virus inert.

"What is it with these people?" Rachel asked to no one in particular. Somehow, her cell phone number had been given out. Someone she was connected to on Facebook had probably sold it to a reporter, and now the phone wouldn't stop ringing. She had to shut it off. Tom's was still on though; he didn't use social networking sites, and was more judicious about giving his number out. At the moment, Rita's fame was undeniable due to the Nobel announcement. Tom figured the fame would be fleeting as Rita's lack of stage presence and outspokenness in the practice of her Catholic faith would soon wear on people. Rita's strategy was simple: she would accept the attention of the limelight that she was normally uncomfortable with in order to build on her name and credibility in medicine. In her acceptance speech, Rita would speak out about the truth surrounding artificial contraception and its dangers. Tom knew that once Rita began using her credibility and fame to expose the truth, the press would drop her like a rock, and the Hollywood AIDS activists, whose lives she had saved would vilify and parody her mercilessly. He knew that people's memories were short once their problems were resolved. In the meantime, they just had to deal with the paparazzi. The reporters knew she was a person of faith and hadn't been able to find any dirt on her because, quite frankly, there wasn't any. But since all of the media types had their own ideas of what being religious meant, and because Rita's interviews thus far were focused on egghead medical concepts that few could understand, they left it alone.

Chapter 26

TIME: "Now"

After filling up her gas tank, (she couldn't remember the last time she filled it completely the price of gas was so crazy) and trying to avoid the hungry stare of the greasy guy filling his truck on the other side of the pump, Rachel drove off to the beach with the radio cranked way up. It was a nice day, maybe 70 degrees, with a light breeze. She drove with both windows down so she could get the full effect of the crosswinds while going over the Intracoastal Waterway. It was fresh enough that you knew it was not summer, but it was by no means cold. It was Saturday, and there was little traffic because the holidays had not started yet. Rachel got to her favorite spot, a semi-secluded area in a less touristy town that did not charge parking fees. She was in luck: all of the spots with a clear view of the water were available.

She parked and turned the engine off but left the radio on. She reached into her handbag and removed the cokes, her cigarette lighter, and her secret stash of generic menthol cigarettes. Rachel was not a big smoker, more of a social smoker when she drank at parties. She'd had this pack for about six months since cigarettes were just too frickin' expensive to smoke with any regularity. With the cigarette lit and the can of coke open, Rachel moved her seat back a little and stared out at the water on the far side of the beach. A nascent breeze blew, varying its intensity from a sweet whisper through the pines to an assertive gust that blew Spanish moss through the air. Staring off into the horizon, Rachel's mind drifted with the music on her favorite 80's station. Tina Turner's tormented refrain kept rolling over and over in her mind as she listened to, 'What's love got to do with it?'

Waxing philosophical, Rachel pondered the idea of 'love'. Had she ever really been in love? She had said those words to a couple of guys in high school, but looking back, she wondered if she had ever meant any of it? Rachel liked getting attention from men, particularly from men who were wanted by other women. To Rachel, it validated her self-image as a powerful woman and gave her a sense of control and victory to know that somebody else's man wanted her. Being desired was very cool, and she

119

had learned to leverage her appearance to achieve those results. But that had nothing to do with love.

Tom liked to tell her that he loved her. At first, it made her feel uncomfortable. She knew that Tom had never been in love, and even if she wasn't sure what love was, she was certain that he didn't either as he had no previous experience in relationships.

So those guys that she had thought she had loved ... one of them had been her first boyfriend, Rod – the one to which she had given her virginity. She thought she loved him, but at fourteen, it was just romanticism. With a single mother working all the time, Rachel had plenty of time to fool around while babysitting her younger sisters. Once Ruth figured it out, she put Rachel on birth control pills. Ruth knew Rachel had her boyfriend over at night when she worked, but didn't mind it at first since Rod had been kind of a tough-guy type, which was a good thing. However, in the long run, it proved counterproductive when they broke up and he began stalking and threatening her to the point where Ruth called the police and they scared him off. *Why is it that most of the guys I find seem to feel like they have to OWN a woman?* Rachel wondered.

Pretty much all the guys she had been with to this point had fit that controlling/possessive profile, except for Tom. Tom was different because he always asked for her opinion about things. At first, she took this as a sign of weakness and indecision on his part, but lately when she took the time to really reflect on his behavior, she had been coming to a different conclusion: the fact that he actually asked her opinion demonstrated that he cared what she thought and valued her ideas. This was respect, something the opposite sex usually failed to show her.

Tom wanted her physically as much as any other guy but he wasn't just looking to use her as a tool for his own gratification or as an ornament on his arm to show off to his friends. No, Tom was genuinely interested in her – Rachel, the person. *So maybe that was love? Or some part of it at least? Maybe he really did know what he was talking about when he told her his feelings.* He wasn't a cool guy by any commonly accepted standard, but he was a real guy, and he always communicated what he thought so she didn't have to guess what was going on in his mind. He was remarkably verbal for a left-brained science nerd. The more she thought about him, the more she smiled. He was 'her' nerd.

Rachel noticed an attractive woman dressed in the same type of 'bad girl' outfit that she was wearing walking past the car. The woman turned briefly and looked at Rachel. She had that same scary black within black look in her eyes that Rachel had seen somewhere before. Yes, Lucy had the same look at the abortion clinic. The disturbing memory made Rachel shiver. The woman stared at Rachel for an uncomfortable period of time as she crossed in front of the car, then continued to a nearby park bench to sit down. Rachel gagged on the putrid stench that blew her way as the woman passed by.

Rachel thought about Tom, and decided to do the Ben Franklin test she had learned from the abortion clinic. So with paper in hand, she wrote down all the reasons to stay with Tom, which took more than a few minutes to accomplish. Things like the way he treated her, the way she felt when they were together, etc. On the other side of the paper, she wrote the opposite. He was a nerd, had no style in clothing, played video games and that was about it. Being honest with herself, Rachel realized that there wasn't very much she didn't like about Tom. She appreciated him, and in her heart admitted that she had no desire to walk away from the relationship they were building. Rachel's musings about Tom were rudely interrupted by a loud double-splat on her windshield. Two seagulls flying overhead contributed their opinions.

"Frickin' great! Thanks, y'all!" she yelled out at the offending birds from the open driver's side window, turning the ignition back on so she could use the washer to clean it up. *Yuck. It didn't clean so well, and some of it was stuck in the cracks and didn't look like it was getting clean. She would have to do it by hand – but later,* she was busy now. She wasn't going to let those slimy critters ruin her creative thought process – not now. Candy had been right about putting things down on paper. It did help to get a perspective on things. *I really do like Tom*; she mused as she put out the remains of her long dead cigarette and

121

slammed the ashtray shut. Sometimes it would pop back out so she needed to hit it twice, usually.

Looking up from the dashboard, she noticed a gaunt, middle-aged man coming down the path, passing the park bench where the attractive and scary woman was seated. The man stared at Rachel with a dark, vacant look in his eyes that was beyond creepy. *Was she seeing things or were his eyes that same black-within-black ..?* He passed her car and leaned against the railing between the path and the beach, acting nonchalant but every now and then looking over at her and fixing his gaze long enough to make her really uncomfortable. This was getting weird. Trying to ignore him, Rachel turned up the radio a little louder and continued what she had been doing.

She took another sip of coke and fumbled around in her purse for that other 'Ben Franklin' list, the one she had completed at the abortion clinic. The song playing on the radio was, 'The Other Side of Life' by the Moody Blues, and she found herself humming along as she reviewed the reasons not to be pregnant now.

It occurred to her that that was kind of an awkward question. Certainly few twenty-year-old college sophomores thought it was a good idea to be pregnant while in school, *so why was the question she answered so skewed? Wouldn't it have been fairer to compare the pluses and minuses of having an abortion? Ah hah! Why would the sales lady who stood to make cash money off her be interested in doing anything to possibly drive away easy money? What would happen in this exercise if she were to re-word the question and get both sides of it?* Right now, she felt like she only had one side of the story.

With a firm sense of purpose, she vigorously tore out a new piece of paper and wrote: <u>Abortion</u> and <u>No Abortion</u> at the top of the two columns. For the abortion side she now had reasons that differed from those she wrote at the clinic. After telling Tom, she realized that 'a guy would ditch her and his responsibilities' certainly didn't fit here. Her list now contained only ten reasons to have an abortion. She noted that it was interesting how, when you changed the wording of the question, it changed the whole balance of the equation; this reminded her of the statistics class she had taken. Feeling really brilliant for figuring out this real life example of something she learned in college, she made a personal commitment, that in the coming days before her next appointment at the clinic, she would get the rest of the information from other sources, starting with the Internet.

She threw all the papers back into her purse, then fumbled around for a stick of gum, and came across the card Ralph had written his contact information on the week before. She took a moment to admire the calligraphic signature, and when she flipped the card over, she noticed that he had written it on the back of Emma's card from Catholic Charities Pregnancy Center. So Ralph knew Emma? He had said the card belonged to a friend, so he probably knew her pretty well. What a small world! Maybe she should ask Emma for some help filling out the other side of the paper she was working on.

Rachel took out her cell phone and dialed the number on Emma's card, and was surprised to hear a familiar voice on the other line. Just then, an old car pulled up in the spot next to her on her passenger side. She wondered why the car parked so close, considering the lot was empty except for her car. There were all kinds of other open parking spaces. Why did this one have to choose to park right next to her? Glancing over, she noticed a man's head through the open window. He turned briefly and stared straight at her with pupil less, black-within black eyes, and didn't turn away. Was she being paranoid, or was there something freaky going on here?

"Emma's line, Ralph here!" a familiar voice replied. Rachel was too startled to hang up and pretend it was a wrong number.

"Oh my gosh! Uncle Ralph? Is that you?"

"Hi Rachel! Great to hear from you! Sometimes when Emma is unavailable her calls get routed to me instead," Ralph said. "It kind of gives her a break sometimes. How're you doing?"

"Doing alright, I guess. I just wanted to get some information from Emma about something."

"Rachel, I'm pretty sure I know why you're calling. I guess congratulations are in order...?" Ralph said with a hint of glee in his voice.

"Uhh, okay. What do you mean by that?" Rachel asked.

"If you're calling Emma's line, chances are that you're pregnant, and given your state of mind the other day, I've got to tell you I'm not surprised." Ralph replied. "Hey, I'm in the area. Can I come over and talk to you?"

"I'm not at home Uncle Ralph," Rachel said a bit hesitantly.

"I know exactly where you are, unless you've sold that LeBaron you had, the one with the dent on the right fender? I can see you from where I am. I'll be there in a minute," Ralph said as he hung up.

Okay, wow. So her secret was out just like that. What would Uncle Ralph say? Surely he would be disappointed in her. Just then a big beautiful luxury car pulled up next to her, and the heavily tinted passenger side window went down to reveal the smiling face of Uncle Ralph.

"Hey Rachel, why don't you lock up the car, and we'll go get a frozen custard? Do you like homemade vanilla? I know a place not far from here that makes the best-frozen custard. It's a quiet place where we can talk and, oh yeah, bring some paper and a pencil because you might want to take some notes," Ralph said.

Rachel followed his instructions and got in his car. As Ralph put the car in reverse, Rachel noticed that all the strange looking people were all staring directly at her with their haunting eyes including another beautiful woman who looked like she must have been the twin sister of the one on the bench.

"Wow, Uncle Ralph, this is an amazing vehicle, and it just feels so nice in here," she said as he pulled out of the parking lot.

"Thanks! It belongs to my boss. It's a one-of-a-kind custom job, and I get to use it when I have an important delivery to make. I was available and in the area when you called, so it worked out," Ralph admitted. "It really is a little piece of heaven, isn't it?"

While Rachel was amazed at the interior and all the options on the dashboard, she just sunk right into the seat. Everything about this vehicle was perfect, and she just felt so peaceful and safe in it. There was a slight scent of flowers emitting from the interior, and the radio was playing some kind of soothing church-type music that was just barely audible, adding to the ambiance of the vehicle.

"Listen, Rachel, I was really happy to be covering Emma's phone when you called. I've always thought you were such a great kid," he admitted.

"And now not so much, huh?" Rachel interrupted.

"No, sweetie, this doesn't change my opinion of you, and I'm not passing judgment. I'm here to help you and your baby by showing you how this seemingly unfortunate turn of events can turn into something wonderful and fulfilling. God can turn any seemingly bad or hopeless situation into a tremendous occasion for blessings – it just takes a little faith and trust, and I know both of those things are in short supply for you right now," Ralph replied softly.

The drive was a short one – perhaps five minutes away. Ralph had been right – it was close. As they turned into the parking lot of the little restaurant, Rachel saw several of the bizarre black-within-black eyed people in the area. One was coming out of the front door, another was on a park bench next to a mother and child who seemed completely unaware of the sinister looking figure seated next to them, and two others were meandering around the parking lot – all of them were staring straight at the

125

car. Seeming to take note of their presence, Ralph offered a suggestion:

"Why don't we just take our custard to go, Rachel? I know a less crowded place we can go to eat them," Ralph said.

"Sure, Uncle Ralph. I don't mind one bit," Rachel replied.

Ralph went to the drive-through window and placed their order. "Two large homemade vanilla custards please," he said to the woman.

Rachel was very focused on the interior of the car – it was awesome to her – but when she glanced out the window, she saw one of the very rough looking, hollow-eyed types staring straight at her with a very dark, menacing expression, and she was glad for the safety of the car.

As if reading her mind, Ralph said, "They can't see you, sweetie. The window tinting totally blocks their view, and they can't touch you when you're with me, so don't worry."

Rachel heard Ralph without completely understanding, but knew intuitively that whatever he said was true. There was clearly something unusual going on around here, and while she didn't get it, she took great comfort in the fact that Ralph did and that he clearly had things under control.

"This is a much rougher area than I thought, Uncle Ralph," Rachel said, looking around.

"Actually, Rachel, this is a very nice area. It's close to the beach and the houses around here start at half a mil and go up from there," he replied.

"Do you live close by, Uncle Ralph?" she asked.

"I stay in a pretty nice place with a lot of other mostly elderly people," he answered enigmatically.

"Oh, I see. One of those – over 55, deed restricted communities?" she guessed. Florida was filled with such developments.

"Well, not exactly, but they are pretty strict about who they'll let in," he replied.

"Uncle Ralph, I've known you for like five or six years now, and I trust you with my life, but I guess I'm so self-absorbed that I've never bothered to find out more about you – even basic information," she said as she ate her ice cream.

"I'm glad to hear you say that you trust me, because, that means I've gotten through to you on some level, and it's really refreshing to hear you analyze your own motivations. I'm guessing it's probably a sign of maturity, plus a byproduct of all the introspective exercises you're doing in those psychology classes. As far as I go, there's not much to tell," Ralph said. "I'm a confirmed bachelor who's married to my work. I don't use the word "married" lightly because I'm totally aware how sacred marriage really is. I love the delivery service that I run; I love my employees and the owner "Mr. J" – my boss who I would do anything for. I really believe that I have found my niche in the organization that he has built. Along the way, in my happy life, I get to meet wonderful people like yourself, and every now and then I get to lend a caring ear or offer some friendly/fatherly advice to people, though what they do with it is ultimately up to them."

This was the most that Rachel had ever heard Uncle Ralph speak about himself, but even now she wasn't sure that she knew a whole lot more about him as a result of the conversation.

"Uncle Ralph, do you have any other family?" she asked inquisitively.

"Well, I'm blessed enough to consider people like you my family," Ralph responded with a smile.

"But I mean parents, brothers, sisters …"

127

"I've never been able to identify any blood relatives per se. I've always figured I was my own species, but if you find any, please tell them to get hold of me," he laughed.

"Okay, Uncle Ralph," Rachel said, deciding to accept his answers at face value and choosing to dig into her ice cream rather than pry any further. Ralph pulled into a church parking lot.

"Here, this is a better spot," he said pulling into a space close by the backside of the church building. "Immaculate Heart Catholic Church is one of my favorites. The pastor here is really good – a very inspiring preacher and an outstanding confessor, even if he has the personality of lawn furniture when he's not doing his job. God Bless him!" Ralph laughed. Rachel looked perplexed at the seeming inconsistency of his last statement.

"Oh, it's okay, Rachel. Old Father Tim and I go back a ways, and he knows I love him, and I know what he thinks of me!" Ralph said, laughing again. "There are a couple of things I want you to see here, so we'll take a look after we finish our treats," he said, rolling down the windows and grabbing his spoon. "MMMMM! Nothing like homemade vanilla!" he said, savoring the richness of his dessert.

"Uncle Ralph, who were all those weird looking people in the parking lots at the beach and ice cream places? I know you knew them or about them. Are they following you around because they recognize your flashy looking car?" Rachel asked.

"No sweetie, they're following you around," he explained.

"Me?" she asked, incredulous. "Is it because of how I'm dressed?" She remembered the leer of the man at the gas station earlier.

"No, Rachel, it's because you're pregnant. Some of them began paying attention to you after you became sexually active, and others came along as the result of other decisions you've made. Still others you picked up at an abortion clinic you must have

128

visited – you can probably recognize those – the more attractive ones with the stench of death around them," Ralph said.

"Why can't I see them now?" she asked, feeling like this conversation was taking a bizarre turn that she was having great difficulty following.

"Well, you can't always see them. In fact, being able to see them is a gift that was given to you at this time for a reason known only to God," Ralph answered. "But they won't come here, not that kind, anyways."

"What do you mean I can't always see them? What are they?" Rachel said, starting to freak out.

"They are our enemies, Rachel. They are the powers and principalities of this present darkness. They are the ones who turned away from God back in the beginning. They hate you and your baby because each of you is made in the image and likeness of their enemy," he explained.

"Why aren't they here now?" Rachel asked, more than a little creeped out by the conversation.

"We're sitting in a parking lot in the back of a chapel. The Eucharist, the very body and blood, soul and divinity of Jesus Christ, is over on the other side of that wall directly in front of us in a tabernacle not ten feet away. There is no place for them here, unless you invite them along," Ralph continued.

"Why would I do that?" Rachel responded, shrugging her shoulders.

"A good question, my dear, and a very fair one. Sometimes it's not just by the act of asking that people invite them along, but by the choices they make in the things that they say and do," Ralph replied.

"You don't seem afraid of them, Uncle Ralph," Rachel said, envying him at this moment.

129

"Why should I be? They don't exist on the same plane of reality as I do or even as you do," Ralph offered. "I can interact with them if there is a reason to do so, but there is absolutely nothing they can do to me."

"Can they hurt me, Uncle Ralph?" Rachel asked nervously.

"Not at the moment. No. But you're not exactly free from them with the lifestyle that you've been leading, and speaking of the way you are dressed ... while that's not the reason they are around you, I would still encourage you to dress more modestly for your own good," Ralph said. "They are not the only ones to fear. When you are ready to make a decision to follow God, you need to get baptized for your own protection."

"MMMMM. This is definitely my favorite by a long shot! I could eat this all day and all night," Ralph said, stuffing some more frozen custard into his cheeks.

Rachel didn't know what to make of all this, and she felt overwhelmed. Being pregnant, on top of having sickly looking weirdos follow her around that apparently were some kind of malevolent spirits, made her more than just nervous – she was a bit confused.

"So, I take it you haven't talked to your mother yet?" Ralph said, changing conversational gears in between spoonfuls of rich, sweet, creamy ice cream.

"No, I've been too afraid of letting her down," Rachel answered with her eyes down. "She's always wanted me to finish school and achieve more than she ever did."

"That's because she's a loving mother. Did you know that your biological father tried to force her to abort you?" Ralph asked, already knowing the answer.

Rachel's jaw dropped, "No! She never told me anything about that!"

"She refused and got some help from my wonderful friends. The same people who are trying to help you. Have you seen the ultrasound yet?" he asked.

"Yes, I've already been over to Emma's. It was pretty impressive what they can do with that machine," Rachel said.

"But it didn't impress you enough to connect with the baby, isn't that right?" Ralph inquired.

"No, it was too small to really see much detail. Ok, I did see the light indicating that the heart was beating, but it was all still kind of abstract to me, and there are so many other things to consider," she responded.

"Like what, for example?" Ralph asked, shoveling more ice cream into his mouth.

"Well, like I'm still in school and I want to finish. I don't want to end up like my mother did, a single mother who works at a club where dirty, creepy, fat guys with no hair and no teeth put their hands all over you for money night after night. I don't want to have to do that," Rachel said with a shiver.

"Well, have you thought of placing the child for adoption? There are many loving families out there that cannot have children of their own and who have to go to foreign countries to get them because most of the unborn are aborted here," Ralph explained. "What about letting the child have a chance at life with someone who will love and take good care of the baby? That would be a very unselfish and heroic thing for a single mother to do if she was not ready to raise a child herself."

"Uncle Ralph, I don't want to be a hero. I know that if I were to carry a child all nine months I would have to keep it," Rachel said with conviction.

"Who would that benefit, though, if you didn't really want the child?" Ralph continued.

131

"I can't explain it, but I know I couldn't give it up if I carried it to term. I think it would just be better to end the pregnancy now," Rachel said. "I'm the woman, it's my choice."

"So then because you couldn't place her for adoption, you think it would be better to kill her? Is that better for her or easier for you? What about her choice? Isn't she a woman too?" Ralph asked.

"Why is it everybody thinks this thing is a girl?" Rachel cried, exasperated. Ralph's questions about her assumptions were right on. She realized she couldn't argue with him, but he wasn't so much arguing as he was turning the things she said around and presenting them in a logical lens through which she hadn't been looking. "It's not fair!"

"You're right, Rachel, it's not fair. Your child has no voice in your decision. You and she have two things in common though. First, neither of you planned to be where you are today, but both of you are there in the same place both literally and figuratively. Second, both of your lives potentially hinge on the decision that you make," Ralph stated.

Rachel's tears were flowing profusely now. "But I was good, I was responsible. I took my pills for protection," Rachel said in a voice filled with grief.

"Rachel, look at me," Ralph said with authority. She raised her eyes to meet his. "You were not supposed to be having sex in the first place. Nobody you trust has ever told you that, so in a way you are not completely responsible, but if you trust in me then hear me now. Sex, and I don't like that word – it's too mechanical – it's real name is "the marriage act", was designed by God to be a great thing to be shared between one man and one woman who have committed their lives completely to each other and to him. Through this act, they communicate their love for one another and for God himself. That love ... that love, Rachel, is a whole other person. This is when humanity is at its most God-like point, when a husband and wife are communicating their love for one another and for God. In a way that parallels the Holy Trinity.

"You see, Rachel," Ralph continued, "God the Father's love for God the Son, and God the Son's love back to God the Father is so complete and total that the love is a third person, God the Holy Spirit. In the Nicene creed we say, 'We believe in the Holy Spirit, the Lord, the Giver of Life, Who proceeds from the Father and the Son, with the Father and the Son he is worshipped and glorified' so when a husband and wife come together it is ordered, it is God-like of them to join together and be open to new life proceeding from their union. In doing this they imitate God, and He is glorified by their unity."

"That third person is the fruit of their commitment, of their love. That is how it was supposed to be from the beginning. That's how human bodies were made to function, not by sharing our most sacred selves with anybody we want at any time just for the pleasure of the moment without being open to the transmission of life."

"Rachel, love is not a feeling. Love is a decision: a commitment of the total giving of oneself to another. Love is patient, love is kind. It is not jealous or pompous, it is not rude, it does not seek its own interests, it is not quick-tempered, it does not hold grudges, it does not rejoice over wrongdoing but rejoices with the truth. It bears all things, believes all things, hopes all things and endures all things. True love never fails and nobody has greater love than the one who would lay their life down for another. Bringing your child to term is an act of true love, and neither you nor your baby deserves anything less than that."

"Even married couples, Rachel, have no business being on the pill, since it causes abortions. The Pro-life people talk about the 1.5 million babies that are killed each year in this country through legal abortion, in which babies are surgically aborted. But often forgotten are untold numbers who die all the time because of the abortafacient nature of hormonal contraception. All chemical contraception is potentially abortafacient when a sexually active woman is ovulating, whether it is through the pill,the implants or the shots. While all of these chemical contraceptives work primarily by tricking the body into thinking it is already pregnant, they also work secondarily by rendering the womb inhospitable to developing life. They do this by thinning the uterine wall to the point where a newly conceived baby cannot implant in her mother's womb. There are tens of millions of abortions that have happened where no one was even aware that they were pregnant. Any woman of childbearing age who engages in the marriage act while she is fertile and on the pill may very well have had one or more abortions already. Don't take my word for it though, the information is out there. Google it for yourself."

"Beyond that Rachel, some barrier contraception, like the IUD, is also abortafacient. In fact, that is the primary way the IUD works – by preventing implantation of a newly conceived child. As for other methods of contraception that are not abortafacient, like condoms and diaphragms, I would ask you to think of it this way. The marriage act is the ultimate form of communication between a husband and wife. How well do you suppose people can communicate if they are wearing a muzzle? It is also holding back, so it is not an act of love, but of lust. In withholding their fertility, the couple says to each other, "Yes, I want to give myself to you, except this other part of me – my fertility." This kind of holding back is selfish and does nothing to promote a healthy union of husband and wife. Communication between two parties, by its very definition, must be open and two-way.

"Rachel, you deserve better than contraception. You deserve the fullness of love that only comes from a covenantal relationship, from marriage. Your unborn daughter deserves a chance to continue her life that began the night she was conceived.

"Sweetie, I can tell you one thing, and that is that the heavens are almost full. God's love is perfect, as is His mercy but He is also perfect in His justice and right now all those children's blood cries out to Him for justice.

"Let's take a walk," Ralph suggested, opening up his car door and coming around to help Rachel with hers.

Ralph held out his hand and helped Rachel up onto the sidewalk that ran around the periphery of the lot where the main church building was. As they passed by the spot where he said the tabernacle was, he made a quick but very reverent bow and she, following, did the same out of respect for him.

134

"There are a couple of things I want you to see," he said, guiding her around the left side of the building towards a solitary tombstone on the grass. Next to the tombstone Rachel saw a well-dressed African-American woman stooped over on a stone bench crying, her head buried in her hands. Around her were three scary, bizarre looking dwarfs with twisted facial features and black- within-black eyes that looked like they were yelling at her. When they looked up and saw Ralph approaching, they fled.

"She brought those tormenters with her, see how cowardly they are?" Ralph said. "They have no hold on her since she's repented of her sins. I hope that now she can begin the rest of the healing process. Why don't you go say hi? I think you know her."

"I don't ..." Rachel stammered as she saw the woman lift her face out from her hands.

"Sandy? Is that you? What happened?" Rachel asked running to sit next to her friend she had met the week before.

"Rachel, O child, I'm so sorry for telling you to have that abortion. Can you ever forgive me?" Sandy asked.

"I haven't done it yet Sandy but why this change of heart and what were you all upset about?"

"Well, after I went in for my pregnancy test last week I found out that I wasn't pregnant so I went to my real doctor and she said that I can't get pregnant because of all the scar tissue from my previous abortions. It turns out there's just no way for a baby to implant in my womb. I went through a whole battery of tests and well ... there's really nothing I can do at this point."

"Oh Sandy I'm so sorry" said Rachel putting her arm around Sandy's shoulder.

"Thanks honey but that's not the worst part. When they were doing all those tests on me they found that my mammogram

135

came back positive, I have breast cancer and it's very advanced, so advanced that I'm not going to have to worry about chemo."

"No! Sandy that's just crazy! How could that all happen?"

"Rachel. It's all my own doing. For years I took all those hormonal contraceptives without ever reading the warning labels or thinking much about it because everybody else was doing it too. The first thing a doctor always asks you when you walk in is 'what kind of birth control do you want?' No one ever told me that there was any danger and I probably wouldn't have believed them if they had. Come to find out that an abortion is also a risk factor for breast cancer; it is one nobody wants to talk about. Hell! The biggest breast cancer research fund raising company flat out denies it on their website so who would know it? But I'm going to die and I feel like I need to at least start being honest with myself about the responsibility that I have for my own health."

"Oh Sandy I'm so sorry. What a terrible burden to carry, no wonder you were crying dear."

"Actually Rachel, I've spent the last few days thinking really hard about my life and the babies I aborted and I've been going to counseling with this nice old priest here, Father Tim," Sandy said, pointing to the Church. "He's been helping me to see the wrongness of the way that I've been living without regard for my family and putting my career before everything else in life. I'm going to die and I can't take my car or anything else that I've worked for with me so none of that really matters, but because of Jesus I now have hope that I may be able to see my babies when I die. Father assured me that they are with God and aren't in any pain. I have named them. I've come to the point where I just realize how wrong I've been and how sorry I am for all that I've done and believe it or not I'm starting to feel more peaceful than I ever have before. I'm going to go home now and talk with my husband and see if I can get him to come with me tomorrow to talk with Father Tim. My husband needs Jesus too; he just doesn't know it yet. Here is my card, call me if you want to talk and please Rachel whatever you do, don't listen to anything I told you before. You have that baby, you hear?" Sandy said as she walked off.

Rachel sat for a moment in stunned silence just trying to process all that she had just seen and heard. She took a moment to stare at the memorial in front of her. It was about two feet long and three feet tall, offset at a 45-degree angle so the lettering could be read without people having to bend down. There was a little badge in one corner that said, 'Knights of Columbus', and the inscription on the stone read:

> IN MEMORY OF THE INNOCENT UNBORN
> VICTIMS OF ABORTION AND THEIR
> SUFFERING PARENTS

"You see, Rachel, the babies aren't the only victims of abortion. Their suffering ends after their dismemberment, but their parents' suffering goes on for the rest of their lives, and even beyond, if they do not deal with what they have done in time," Ralph added somberly as he came up and sat next to her.

"Rachel, you're better than this, and so is your baby. C'mon, I have one last thing I want to show you. It's on the other side of the building. Then I'll take you back to your car. The enemies will be gone when we get back there," he added knowingly as he led her around the other side of the church to a shrine. It was a tasteful, black relief carving on a white stone of a kneeling woman. Presumably, it was the Virgin Mary, looking at an angel, who had appeared above her.

"Do you remember what I told you the other night after dinner about Mary?" Ralph asked. "I thought you might like to see this beautiful representation of Mary saying 'yes' to God's messenger. Somehow I don't think the Angel Gabriel would look quite as sissified as the artist made him look in this picture, and those wings are just way too big," Ralph laughed as he continued. "And pretty as this image of the Virgin Mary is, I'm sure it doesn't do her justice. But when you think about it, isn't it just awe-inspiring? I mean, here is this totally innocent young Jewish girl being told by a heavenly being that the Holy Spirit was going to overshadow her and make her pregnant with God's

137

only Son, and all she has to do is say 'no,' and it won't happen, but she doesn't. She trusts God and accepts His will for her completely, even though from her perspective, she can't really see how it's all going to work out. Since she's engaged to Joseph and they haven't touched each other. I mean, she's got to be thinking 'the villagers and even my own family will stone me' because that was the penalty for getting pregnant out of wedlock. But she looks beyond the darkness and trusts God with her whole self, with her very life, and in so doing, she gains his own life forever!"

"Rachel, be like Mary. God is reaching out to you now, asking you to trust Him. He's putting before you life and death. Now choose life so that you and your babies will live," and with that, Ralph didn't say anything more. He had delivered the message: now she needed time to think about what he had said. He turned and took her hand and led her back to the car in silence, opening the passenger door for her before getting back in on the driver's side.

They drove back in silence. Rachel felt like talking would have been inappropriate. She had nothing to say, really, but a lot to think about. As they were driving back, Rachel's gaze moved around the interior of the car and noticed something peculiar that had escaped her notice before – the steering wheel that Ralph was holding did not seem to be physically connected to the dashboard or any kind of steering column that she could see. Either it was some kind of optical illusion, a custom attribute of this amazing vehicle, or she was going nuts.

Oh great, now I'm seeing things, she thought. Ralph briefly looked over at her and winked as if reading her thoughts, but he didn't say a word. When they got back to the beach parking lot, it was just as Ralph had said. The creepy types were all gone. They were the only people there. It had cooled down a few degrees and the sun was getting ready to set; gentle breezes moved the Queen palm fronds back and forth.

"Thanks for everything, Uncle Ralph, you're the best. We've got to get together again soon!" she said, breaking the silence.

"That's entirely up to you, my dear. Just know that I love you and Rita both, and help is only a phone call away. Please give my love to your parents. I prayed for traveling mercies for you so you will make it back home safely, but you need to have your battery checked. It's not a new car, and you can't use the radio with the engine turned off like you were doing, okay?" he said. Rachel nodded, and Ralph put the window back up and took off. *Hey how did he know about the name Rita? Did I say something to him about that? I don't think I did,* she wondered as she got in her car, enjoying the feeling of the solid 'THUMP' as it closed behind her on the first attempt, The motor took an extra couple seconds but it did start up the first time and inexplicably, the windshield was completely clean.

On the ride home, Rachel was almost on autopilot. She hadn't fully assimilated all the events of the day. Things certainly hadn't gone the way she had anticipated when she left the house this morning. She tried not to think about her conversation with Uncle Ralph, and instead concentrated on the beauty of the light reflecting on the water and the bridges during the sunset hour, while trying to stay focused on her driving. She sang along with her favorite 80's radio station without realizing it, and caught herself singing along with Madonna's 'Papa Don't Preach, I've made up my mind, I'm keeping my baby ...' *oh wait, what?!*

Wow that was funny, she thought, laughing to herself as she drove the rest of the way home.

139

Chapter 27

TIME: "Now"

Walking into her house, she found that the place was empty. Whenever you walked into the house and the TV was not on it meant that no one was home. The television and computer were the family's biggest forms of entertainment. They only had one TV, and could record programs to watch later but it was part of a digital fiber optic service package that also gave them high-speed internet. The family had worked out a schedule of who got to watch their shows when, which Rachel had opted out of when she graduated from high school since she wasn't around much of the time.

A note on the computer monitor told her that the rest of the family had gone out to the drive-in and that there was some fried chicken in the refrigerator for her. Flicking on the TV set more out of habit than out of interest, Rachel went to her room to change into her comfortable sweats. She grabbed the mostly – empty bucket of chicken and a diet soda from the fridge, and sat herself down at the computer to check her e-mail and Facebook accounts while the TV commentator droned on about something she couldn't care about.

Checking her e-mail first, she saw that she had a few offers for bizarre products and services in her junk folder, and a load of notifications from Facebook that she had pending messages from her friends. She switched to Facebook and began catching up. She got an Instant Message right away from someone she didn't feel like talking to, so she put herself in off-line mode and decided to catch up on her e-mail and posts undistracted.

Let's see, a message from Suzy – no make that three messages from Suzy, all within the last eight hours; a message from Greta about getting together tonight – ooops too late for that one! Hit delete; a message from Brad – what is he writing for? He is the jerk who dumped me. Looks like he's trolling for a date ... nope, sorry Brad, should have de-friended you a long time ago. You're gone, goodbye; an invitation to take an 'I am a moron test' – boring, no thanks, delete; an invitation to find our which of Abe

Lincolns relatives you were in a past life – stupid, no thanks, delete; three invitations to a virtual lollypop party – no thanks, delete; an invitation to watch the grass grow on a virtual reality site – where do they come up with this trash? Delete; a message from one of Tom's loser friends asking if it was true that we were breaking up? What? Where is that coming from? Oh, and here is another one from one of my friends asking the same thing? What is going on here?

On and on Rachel poured through the messages and notifications she had gotten from some of her 1200 'friends' that day. Most of the messages she deleted because the 'friend' wasn't that interesting to her, but she was too lazy to de-friend them. When she had first opened her Facebook account, she had put a picture of herself in a bikini as her profile picture. It had been the same one that she used on MySpace, but her MySpace profile had been closed off to people that she didn't know because she was under 18 when she had opened it and never changed the settings. Within a couple of days she had 500 new 'friends,' most of them men. Her girlfriend had helped her to whittle through the list to delete all the ones they thought were losers based on their profiles and pictures. Then she started getting cell phone calls from some of them, and since then she had been more selective about who she friended.

Then she looked at Tom's loser friend Harold's message asking if it was true that they were no longer together, and if not would she go out with him … *what a dork!* she thought. *Not only wasn't he getting a reply, he was getting de-friended and blocked!*

Okay, so what's this about Tom and I breaking up? Hhhhmmmmm…not much information, just a straightforward inquiry from Simone. Rachel fired off a reply saying, "No, not that I'm aware of … where did this information come from?" She looked at Tom's profile and saw that instead of being listed as 'in a relationship with Rachel Perdue,' the status had been changed to 'it's complicated.' *What was he thinking?*

She looked again through her e-mails and didn't see any communication from him, and wondered, *where did he get off thinking that he could break up with her?* Then she remembered

141

that she had been blowing him off and not taking any of his calls for the first part of the week. She always felt like she was in control of the relationship and he was just like her little lap puppy, but now he was going public with their problems. Not good.

Rachel got out her cell and tried to call him, but the phone just rang into voice-mail, which really upset her. So she tried two more times before finally leaving a message, saying, "Tom Pierce, you need to call me right away and explain yourself!" She was not used to not getting her way with him, and for a girl who had always counted on her looks to get her what she wanted, there was no worse feeling than being ignored. Trying not to think about it, she looked at her own status, which just showed 'pending' and went ahead and changed it to 'single.'

"There, let him deal with that!" she said, calling his bluff, knowing that it would instantly be all over their common 'friends' walls.

Come to think of it, she should have let that Harold dweeb get that before she deleted him. No, a better idea would have been to forward his inquiry about her status to Tom to remind him that he wasn't the only one – although he knew she didn't like Harold, so maybe it was just as well that she did already delete his message.

So, Tom was growing a pair and standing up to her. *Maybe it is time for us to part,* she mused, not really meaning it, but trying to practice putting on her best poker face for when she did get to talk to him. One thing was for sure, if his goal was to get her attention, it had worked.

Rachel was frustrated and tired. It had been a long day, and she didn't feel like dealing with anything else right now. She was emotionally drained and her brain was fried. Even the bucket of chicken wasn't enough to keep her up; rather, it had the opposite effect making her want to sleep. She was ready to give in to the sandman's advances. Leaving the TV running, she put away the last piece of chicken and went to bed. Within minutes, her day was finished.

Chapter 28

TIME: "Eternity"

Tammy understood what was going on since she could see it from all sides until this juncture. God's revelation to her was complete, and she saw things through His eyes until this point in time. That she was focused in on this moment in linear time was an indication that He wanted her to pray specifically for this situation, and she was overjoyed to be able to do so. What a privilege the Almighty gave her to allow her to ask Him for His favor for situations in the lives of those who came after her in time! She knew everything about her lost daughter Ruth, and granddaughters, and everything about everyone in each of their lives. She knew them better than they knew themselves, since she was sharing God's beatific vision. What unspeakable joy! What bliss to know that the Creator thought so much of her that He wanted to involve her and let her play a role in building up her family and friends who were still back in time! Tammy was awash with love and gratitude.

"Oh my Beloved, hear my plea for my grandchildren. Have mercy on them, for they never knew You. Show Yourself to them in a new way, my Love, open their hearts to Your heart and to Your word, give them eyes to see and ears to hear what You have in store for those who love You. Spirit of Love, give them the mind of Jesus and teach them Your wisdom, Tammy prayed, but even as she prayed she felt the prayers of others joined with hers: the kindly mailman she had known growing up, her mother and her grandparents, her first grade teacher, and Rachel's cheerleading coach from high school who had joined heaven after a car accident. All of these hearts, and many more, all prayed together in unity with Tammy. It was a great symphony of harmonious prayer and love – it was wondrous and beautiful to behold and participate in, and Jesus was the great conductor of it all. Her beloved heard her and promised her He would fulfill her request, and asked her to continue her great work of mercy by persevering in prayer for Rachel, Tom, and Rita. Since she was complete in Him, she could not refuse, and indeed had no inkling of what it might mean to refuse Him. He was her constant ever-present love and her existence. She knew He would do as He said, and she rejoiced in His love and His mercy.

Chapter 29

TIME: "Now – A Day Later"

"Rachel!" the lady with the clipboard called into the stuffy waiting room. Rachel followed her into a room that she hadn't seen before. Judging by the dimensions, it must have been one of the larger operating rooms.

"Go ahead and put this gown on, the doctor will be in here in a few minutes. There won't be a long wait today. Sharrie is coming in to take your blood pressure. You paid for the anesthesia? Good move!" she said, smiling.

Two other figures were in the room unseen by anyone else. If anyone could have seen them, they would have looked liked a very handsome couple.

"This is where it happens," Lucy hissed excitedly. "You lost again!" she gloated at Gabe, whose presence she loathed and resented. She just hoped he didn't start reciting the words of her enemy, but she knew there was nothing she could do to stop that from happening.

Undressed and exposed in the stirrups, Rachel counted backwards from 10 until she fell asleep. Rachel's breathing was mechanical and rhythmic as Sharrie held the anesthesia mask and breathing tube in place.

"What a treasure the world is losing, and they'll never know in this life," Gabe eulogized." My people perish for want of knowledge ... one and all they sin against Me, exchanging their glory for shame."

"You don't belong here! This one's mine, you gave her every chance and she rejected your God. She belongs to me now – it was her choice." Lucy cackled with delight at the irony of the wonderful 'choice' deception her minions had succeeded in selling to the human population thousands of times each day.

145

"Yes, she's all yours by an act of will, but not for another few minutes. I'm here for Rita. She's innocent; you have no claim to her." This was not an isolated incident, as tens of thousands of babies were being slaughtered each day through abortion and chemical contraception. Gabe was his boss' number one messenger, and was only used for the most important cases. Due to the special nature of this child, whom God had sent in response to hundreds of millions of prayers for an end to A.I.D.S., Gabe himself was here to receive this special soul. It really grated at Lucy that she could do nothing to stop this unborn child from spending the rest of eternity with her sworn enemy and his Son. Her small consolation was that the baby's little body would soon be sold to a cosmetics company and ground up to make collagen so that some other woman's vanity could be appeased. Deep down, Lucy knew her limitations; she was after all only a created entity herself, and could not really operate without the direct cooperation of human beings. The only power she really had was that which they gave her. The one she had declared to be her enemy, ironically, her creator too, was under no such restriction.

"Okay, Gabe, you want to watch how it happens? You get a front row seat to this one," Lucy said, walking around to speak in the doctor's ear. "**D and C!**"

"Sharrie, let's go green today. We'll save some electricity and give the vacuum a rest and do a D and C abortion this time," Dr. Cutter said cheerily as if receiving a sudden spark of inspiration. "Do you remember what we use for one?"

"Yes, Doctor, we used the knifey-thing with the loop on it, and I have to wear gloves, but I already got some on – see?" she said, showing him her hands covered in stained latex.

"Very good, Sharrie. The knifey-thing is called a curette; did you remember to run the other one under hot water like I told you? No? Why don't you do that now. Put some of that disinfectant soap on it too." Laide's cost cutting strategies sometimes meant they did not have enough sterilized equipment toward the end of the month, forcing him to improvise with soap and water. "And do feel free to use the restroom before we get started. Oh that is awful," he said, holding his nose and grabbing frantically for a

146

bottle of Lysol, spraying in vain many times around the little room. He had to bring the Lysol from home because Laide was too cheap to provide it. It always stunk in this place. He went through a can a day and it never quite seemed to do the trick.

They had a good crowd in the waiting room today, and Ike Cutter had big plans to visit a special underground massage parlor with his oldest and best friend Elmer tonight. At Ike's age, he was way passed getting what he wanted without paying for it, and tonight he would have all the cash he needed to have the best possible time! In order to get there, though, he had to get through that whole waiting room filled with women and girls, and that meant going a little faster than usual. Quickly, he dilated her cervix.

Rachel was out cold so he didn't have to worry about softening it up first. She would feel pain later on anyway, and would just think that it had to do with the procedure itself. Then he inserted the curette and began scraping the uterus wall. On his first pass he got about half of Rita's little body. He kept scrapping, and on his second withdrawal found most of the rest. Somehow, it looked like maybe he had missed the head that time. He was doing well for time but really wanted to see if he could finish this one ahead of schedule. Reaching in again he scrapped some more and got distracted by a loud monotone humming coming from the respirator.

"Doctor, why is that machine making the noise?" asked Sharrie.

Looking at the machine, Cutter saw the flat line.

"Ah *$%^!" the abortionist exclaimed, pulling out the curette with the wrong colored substances on it. "Effed up another one! Laide! Help me out here! I've got a bleeder! CODE DOUBLE RED, LAIDE! DOUBLE RED!!"

In the course of scraping her womb, he had punctured it, which was easy to do, and surprisingly, it did not happen more often. By the color of the substances coming out of Rachel, he knew that he had torn into her colon, and she was hopelessly infected at this point. What's worse, she had an adverse reaction to the anesthesia, which is what was causing her to flat line – must

147

have had low blood pressure or something. *Geez, didn't Laide even check for that anymore,* he wondered.

The chart said 120 over 80, but clearly by her reaction to the anesthesia that could not have been the case. This one was gone, but now he had to figure out a way to make it look like it wasn't his fault, and Laide was really good at that. It would all be over for this poor girl in a matter of minutes. Same routine as before, they would fix her up as best they could to make it look like it had occurred naturally, then they would call the private ambulance to pick up the body. Laide paid the private ambulance service a monthly fee NOT to turn on the sirens and lights whenever they came to pick one up. May as well take her off the anesthesia and save Laide some money.

There she stood in a tribute to what she was meant to be – Rita, named after the patron saint of impossible causes. Rita, chosen by God the Father in response to millions of prayers for an end to A.I.D.S. She looked timeless, perhaps thirty years old if you tried to put a number on her age, and she shone so brilliantly that Lucy was forced to cover her eyes. "Ahhhh," she gagged.

In the light of Rita's radiance, Lucy no longer appeared to be a beautiful woman but a grossly disfigured being more reptilian or insectoid than human in appearance. The light that reflected off of Rita was a pure innocence, a reflection of the light of the world, Jesus Christ, and Lucy could not bear it. She tried to shield herself by looking away, but she could feel the light's warmth on her extremities, and it filled her with revulsion. She was powerless to stop this torment since it came from a source that was not created and that she had no power over. Yes, Rita's body was dead, but Rita had died without sin, an innocent victim of convenience and self-will. Now she was a ward of God's mercy. The pain of dismemberment was over and the memory erased.

"Rita, I am here to take you to a safe place, but I need you to stay here for a few moments longer. You won't be able to hear or see anything, but this is God's will."

Rita, now protected by God's mercy, was incapable of anything but complete obedience and trust in Gabriel and the words he

148

spoke. *"Yes, Gabriel,"* she smiled sweetly, not understanding but not worried, completely at peace and without fear.

Rachel awoke and knew total fear. This fear went way beyond the angst she had felt earlier in the day. That was just nervousness at an impending event that you knew would be over at some point ... this was different ... she found herself drowning in waves of hopeless desperation. There was no sense at all that there would ever be any conceivable relief from it or that it was her only problem ... she sat up and noticed that her body did not follow her.

"Oh God, I'm dead!" she realized, and glancing ahead where a beautiful woman figure might have been she saw the most hideous and fearsome creature dripping and oozing all manner of vile pus and filth from every orifice staring straight at her. Was it smiling?

"Good job, Rachel! You were given every opportunity to turn away from this choice and still you chose to do it your way – I mean 'my way.' Hey, would you like to sing a little song with me before I drag you to your new home?" Lucy's familiar voice snickered from the disfigured beast who exuded nothing but malicious intent and the foulest stench. *"C'mon, let's do a duet. I'll start...I did it MY WAYYY ..."* Lucifer sang mockingly.

Overwhelmed with terror and grief, Rachel caught sight of Gabe, but he was not paying attention to her. He was giving some instructions to a beautiful creature filled with light. *"Gabe! Gabe, can you help me?"* she yelled, but intuitively knew the answer even as she asked the question.

"I'm sorry, Rachel," he said, and waving his hand in front of her she was given a moment to reflect on the sum totality of her life – each moment and all together at the same time. She saw how each decision she made had affected everything else, how each sin, every lie, every false witness, every impurity had affected not just her own self but the people around her. Rachel saw the son she never knew she had conceived with her first boyfriend. In their youthful lust they had created him unawares, but as a side effect of the birth control pills she took, he had never been able

149

to implant in her womb properly, so he had been aborted – a tragic, senseless loss.

Then she saw Rita standing there in all her perfection, and beneath her timeless adult form she saw Rita's tiny body parts in the bin on the table covered in blood – both hers and Rachel's – a cruel mockery of what was supposed to have been.

In a flash, Rachel saw God's entire plan for Rita's life, all the good she would have done, the millions of lives she would have saved. She saw too all the blessings that she had given up. She saw the joys and triumphs that she would never know, and felt the loss of each one. The tender, nurturing love of a husband, the love of children and family, the personal and professional successes she was supposed to have had, the Nobel prize for Rita, the grandchildren and great grandchildren who were supposed to open presents at her house on Christmas and gather around the table at Thanksgiving and Easter. She would miss the happy times, such as the baptisms, first communions, confirmations, the weddings and graduations that now would never be, and most of all the love of Jesus that she had shunned time after time.

God had done everything possible to get her attention, she saw that now. She knew it then, but she just didn't want to hear it. He even sent His only son Jesus to die in her place, and she had, by her decisions and actions, pulled Him off the cross that had been meant for her and placed herself back on it in vain. In that moment, that instant, she heard Gabe's warning that he had given her the other day in front of the abortion clinic:

"Jesus Christ loves you and Rita both, and He wants you to know that He has everything taken care of if you will just trust Him." She had ignored it. Now it was too late, and she had eternity to think about it.

"It is finished," Gabriel said, taking Rita in his holy embrace and disappearing while Rachel mourned.

"Hey, you like old music. I know a great tune that would be appropriate right now," Lucifer shrieked with pleasure as her clawed hands tore into Rachel. "You and me together forever ..."

150

"AAAAAAAAHHHHH!!!!"

Denouement

Rachel woke up in a cold sweat; her pink flowered nightgown was soaked from wetting the bed as well. Rachel climbed out of her soiled sheets and fell to her knees sobbing like a baby. The light went on in the room; it was Maggie, and she was awake.

"Oh God, Maggie! I really screwed up this time..."

From her place in heaven, Tammy said, "The enemy is there. Pray, now Maggie!"

Maggie had a moment of inspiration and prayed, *"In the name of Jesus, I bind any evil spirits that come against my family!* What is it sissy? What's wrong? Oh, you wet the bed...." she said, seeing the wet nightgown clinging to her sister's legs.

"No, Maggie, it's much worse ... I .... I'm pregnant, and I dreamed that I had abortions and it was awful, so much worse than just being pregnant," Rachel continued.

"Oh sissy! How far along are you?" Maggie said as she too got on the floor to embrace her troubled sister.

"Eight weeks," she sobbed.

"There, there, honey, it'll be okay. We'll all get through it," Maggie said as she held her sister.

"What happened? Is everything okay, girls?" Ruth asked, walking into the room while wrapping a bathrobe around herself.

"Oh Mom, I'm so sorry. I got pregnant. I know how much you wanted me to do well in school. I was going to have an abortion,

152

but ...," Rachel couldn't continue as the tears flowed down her face.

"No," Ruth said firmly. "No woman in this family is going to submit to any abortion. I don't have all the answers. Heck I'm not even smart enough to even ask the right questions, but I know one thing, and that is I love my children and I will love my grandchildren, and nobody, not even you," she said, pointing her finger at Rachel, "are going to cut any of them up while I am around. Is that clear?"

Unseen by the women, two other figures were in the room with them – one of them a nice older man they would have been very familiar with if he were visible, the other a demented dwarf sitting on the floor with his hands and feet bound.

"Let me go, Ralph! This is my domain, you @#% %%#$!" Asmo screamed as if in excruciating pain.

"You really were the best of the dream weavers, Asmo. By the way, thanks for the help tonight. You were so into the pain and grief you were causing Rachel that you scared her right into the Boss' arms. Good work! So, how does it feel to work for the Man?" laughed Ralph.

"She's still mine!" Asmo claimed.

"Yeah, sure, buddy, for about three more minutes. Then she gives her life to Him and gets a guardian. Hmmm, I wonder who they'll assign to keep you at bay?" Ralph mused.

"My @#$%^ hands hurt! I thought you %@## were supposed to be merciful!" Asmo moaned.

Crying, Ruth bent over to join her two oldest daughters in a group hug. "It's 5:30 a.m. already. I'm going to make us some coffee. Maggie, why don't you help your sister to get cleaned up?" Ruth suggested, and so the women stayed up to watch the sunrise together. Taking a sip of coffee, Maggie felt inspired to share something she had read with Rachel and Ruth. It was from her bible. From 2 Chronicles 7:14:

> If my people, upon whom my name has been
> pronounced, humble themselves and pray, and
> seek my presence and turn from their evil ways,
> I will hear them from heaven and pardon their
> sins and revive their land.

"Well, I'm ready to pray, Maggie. I need help, and I don't really know how, so you have to show me," Rachel said.

"Gladly, sis," Maggie answered.

And with that, Maggie prayed out loud and signaled for when her mother and sister should join in. Then she opened the scriptures to them, and for the first time shared of the new life, she had found in Christ. Ruth wasn't sure about it all, but she saw that Rachel was really drinking it up, so she just stayed quiet and listened to the interaction between her daughters.

Two hours later, Rachel got out her cell phone and called Tom.

"Hey," she said.

"Hey yourself," he replied. "It's kind of early. What's going on?" he asked, trying hard to sound casual and nonchalant.

"I'm going to have the baby. We need to talk."

"Ok, let me grab a shower first," Tom said before hanging up.

Forty minutes later there was an expected knock at the door, Rachel ran to let Tom in and saw that he had a cardboard box with him.

"Hey babe," he said, kissing her long and hard. "I missed you."

"You sure played it cool this time, Tom. You had me worried that you weren't going to keep me around. "It's complicated, huh?" she said, looking into his eyes.

"I learned from the best," he replied with a Cheshire grin. Rachel sat down on a chair and Tom pulled up in front of her on his knees, still kissing her intermittently.

"So what's in the box?" she asked, breaking the mood.

"Oh, this" he said, pulling it around next to him. "Well, Christmas time is coming up and I seem to remember hearing a story about three wise men bringing gifts. So me, myself and I decided to wise up and each bring you a gift," he said, reaching into the box to pull out the first one. This present was small and the wrapping was way too tidy, so there was no way he did it himself. Rachel noted that it was in the shape of a jewelry box, so it was probably expensive. She opened it up and saw a gold diamond engagement ring. "This one is from me," he said. It wasn't big but she loved it immediately.

"Oh Tom," Rachel said, wrapping her arms around his neck.

"Don't say anything yet, Rachel, just hear me out. I'm probably not the guy you always saw yourself with, but I have to believe there is something about me that you are attracted to because you are a woman with options, and you could be with any guy, but you chose to be with me," Tom said. "I love you with all my heart and I want to make a life with you and with our child. I know that just because we're having a baby doesn't mean that we should get married, but I think in our case the timing will work out well enough. I will take care of things and I will never betray your trust in me. I am giving you this ring whether you agree to marry me or not. I would ask, though, that you put it on your right hand as a 'promise ring' until you are ready to say 'yes' to marrying me. The promise being that I will wait until you are ready."

Tears came back to Rachel's bloodshot eyes. She took a look at the ring, and without hesitation put it on the ring finger of her left hand. "I love you, Tom Pierce, and yes, I will marry you," she said as they embraced and kissed deeply. After a tender

155

moment with both of them in tears, Rachel asked expectantly, "So what else is in the box?"

"Just a couple of things I thought you would really like," he said, bringing out two more boxes. These presents both had weird wrapping paper and the seams were tied with duct tape. *He must have got these at Wal-Mart and wrapped them himself,* she figured, smiling in between teardrops in anticipation and giggling at his silly wrapping job. She fumbled through the duct tape and opened up the little necklace-type jewelry box to find ... her mother-daughter twin heart pendant that she had pawned. When she opened it up, she found two pictures, one of her as she was now and the other of Tom. So if this was her locket, then the big one must be ... "Rita!!" she exclaimed, bursting open the package and bawling like a baby holding the doll she had treasured for most of her life and almost lost forever in a moment of short-sightedness.

"That one was picked out all by myself," he said, completing his play on words. Looking up at Tom, her puzzled expression asked what the lump in her throat would not let her verbalize.

"Julia at the pawn shop is one of my classmates in engineering. She recognized you from campus and called me to let me know what you'd done yesterday. I was going to wait until Christmas, but since I'm laying it all on the line with you today, I decided not to hold back," Tom said. "Say, that sounds like a pretty good name for a girl. What do you think? Rita."

"Rita, Rita, Rita.... hhhmmm that's not impossible..."

For further reference and reflection

Enter any of the terms below in your internet search engine

Theological Teachings

Humanae Vitae by Pope Paul IV

Catechism of the Catholic Church #2331-2400

Evangelium Vitae by Pope John Paul II

Practical Resources for Natural Family Planning

Creighton Model NFP

Couple to Couple League / Sympto-thermal NFP

La Leche League

Other Organizations

Priests for Life

The Center for Bio-Ethical Reform

Human Life International

Life Dynamics – Lime 5

American Life League

Help for a Crisis Pregnancy

National Life Center 1-800-848-LOVE

Birthright 1-800-550-4900

Option Line 1-800-395-HELP

Post Abortion Healing

Rachel's Vineyard Retreats

157

Made in the USA
Charleston, SC
23 October 2016